THERE'S SOMETHING STRANGE about the new girls in town. Briar Creek, Oregon, has never seen anything like the supernatural grace of Rowan, Kestrel, and Jade, three sisters who move into the dilapidated old house next to Mark and Mary-Lynnette Carter.

Mark is obsessed with Jade—but she and her sisters have a secret. And when Mark and Mary-Lynnette follow them into the woods one night, they are plunged into a nightmare beyond their imagination.

Because the sisters are fugitives from the Night World, and their brother, Ash, is hot on the trail behind them. He's ruthless, he's gorgeous, and he has orders to bring the girls back at all costs. And when he sees Mary-Lynette, he decides to take her, too. . . .

DAUGHTERS OF DARKNESS

THE NIGHT WORLD SERIES

• •

Night World

Daughters of Darkness

Spellbinder

Dark Angel

The Chosen

Soulmate

Huntress

Black Dawn

Witchlight

NIGHT WORLD · BOOK TWO

DAUGHTERS OF DARKNESS

L. J. SMITH

SIMON PULSE
NEW YORK LONDON TORONTO SYDNEY NEW DELHI

This book is a work of fiction. Any references to historical events, real people, or real places are used fictitiously. Other names, characters, places, and events are products of the author's imagination, and any resemblance to actual events or places or persons, living or dead, is entirely coincidental.

SIMON PULSE

An imprint of Simon & Schuster Children's Publishing Division

1230 Avenue of the Americas, New York, New York 10020

This Simon Pulse hardcover edition December 2016

For information about special discounts for bulk purchases, please contact Simon & Schuster Special Sales at 1-866-506-1949 or business@simonandschuster.com.

The Simon & Schuster Speakers Bureau can bring authors to your live event. For more information or to book an event contact the Simon & Schuster Speakers Bureau at 1-866-248-3049 or visit our website at www.simonspeakers.com.

Cover designed by Regina Flath

Interior designed by Mike Rosamilia

The text of this book was set in Adobe Garamond.

Manufactured in the United States of America

2 4 6 8 10 9 7 5 3 1

Library of Congress Control Number 2016948190

ISBN 978-1-4814-7964-6 (hc)

ISBN 978-1-4814-7965-3 (eBook)

In memory of
John Manford Divola

And for Julie Ann Divola,
still the best of best friends

CHAPTER 1

Rowan, Kestrel, and Jade," Mary-Lynnette said as she and Mark passed the old Victorian farmhouse.

"Huh?"

"Rowan. And Kestrel. And Jade. The names of the girls who're moving in." Mary-Lynnette tilted her head toward the farmhouse—her hands were full of lawn chair. "They're Mrs. Burdock's nieces. Don't you remember I told you they were coming to live with her?"

"Vaguely," Mark said, readjusting the weight of the telescope he was carrying as they trudged up the manzanita-covered hill. He spoke shortly, which Mary-Lynnette knew meant he was feeling shy.

"They're pretty names," she said. "And they must be sweet girls, because Mrs. Burdock said so."

"Mrs. Burdock is crazy."

"She's just eccentric. And yesterday she told me her nieces

are all beautiful. I mean, I'm sure she's prejudiced and everything, but she was pretty definite. Each one of them gorgeous, each one a completely different type."

"So they should be going to California," Mark said in an almost-inaudible mutter. "They should be posing for *Vogue.* Where do you want this thing?" he added as they reached the top of the hill.

"Right here." Mary-Lynnette put the lawn chair down. She scraped some dirt away with her foot so the telescope would sit evenly. Then she said casually, "You know, I thought maybe we could go over there tomorrow and introduce ourselves—sort of welcome them, you know. . . ."

"Will you cut it *out*?" Mark said tersely. "I can organize my own life. If I want to meet a girl, I'll meet a girl. I don't need help."

"Okay, okay. You don't need help. Be careful with that focuser tube—"

"And besides, what are we going to say?" Mark said, on a roll now. "'Welcome to Briar Creek, where nothing ever happens. Where there are more coyotes than people. Where if you *really* want some excitement you can ride into town and watch the Saturday night mouse racing at the Gold Creek Bar. . . .'"

"Okay. Okay." Mary-Lynnette sighed. She looked at her younger brother, who just at the moment was illuminated by the last rays of sunset. To see him now, you'd think he'd never been sick a day in his life. His hair was as dark and shiny as Mary-Lynnette's, his eyes were as blue and clear and snapping. He had the same healthy tan as she did; the same glow of color in his cheeks.

But when he'd been a baby, he'd been thin and scrawny and every breath had been a challenge. His asthma had been so bad he'd spent most of his second year in an oxygen tent, fighting to stay alive. Mary-Lynnette, a year and a half older, had wondered every day if her baby brother would ever come home.

It had changed him, being alone in that tent where even their mother couldn't touch him. When he came out he was shy and clingy—holding on to their mother's arm all the time. And for years he hadn't been able to go out for sports like the other kids. That was all a long time ago—Mark was going to be a junior in high school this year—but he was still shy. And when he got defensive, he bit people's heads off.

Mary-Lynnette wished one of the new girls *would* be right for him, draw him out a bit, give him confidence. Maybe she could arrange it somehow. . . .

"What are you thinking about?" Mark asked suspiciously.

Mary-Lynnette realized he was staring at her.

"About how the seeing's going to be really good tonight," she said blandly. "August's the best month for starwatching; the air's so warm and still. Hey, there's the first star—you can make a wish."

She pointed to a bright point of light above the southern horizon. It worked; Mark was distracted and looked, too.

Mary-Lynnette stared at the back of his dark head. If it would do any good, I'd wish for romance for you, she thought.

I'd wish it for myself, too—but what would be the point? There's nobody around here to be romantic *with.*

None of the guys at school—except maybe Jeremy Lovett—understood why she was interested in astronomy, or what she felt about the stars. Most of the time Mary-Lynnette didn't care—but occasionally she felt a vague ache in her chest. A longing to . . . share. If she *had* wished, it would have been for that, for someone to share the night with.

Oh, well. It didn't help to dwell on it. And besides, although she didn't want to tell Mark, what they were wishing on was the planet Jupiter, and not a star at all.

Mark shook his head as he tramped down the path that wound through buckbrush and poison hemlock. He should have apologized to Mary-Lynnette before leaving—he didn't *like* being nasty to her. In fact, she was the one person he usually tried to be decent to.

But why was she always trying to *fix* him? To the point of wishing on stars. And Mark hadn't really made a wish, anyway. He'd thought, If I was making a wish, which I'm not because it's hokey and stupid, it would be for some excitement around here.

Something wild, Mark thought—and felt an inner shiver as he hiked downhill in the gathering darkness.

Jade stared at the steady, brilliant point of light above the southern horizon. It was a planet, she knew. For the last two nights she'd seen it moving across the sky, accompanied by tiny pinpricks of light that must be its moons. Where she came from, nobody was in the habit of wishing on stars, but this planet seemed like a friend—a traveler, just like her. As Jade watched it tonight, she felt a sort of concentration of hope rise inside her. *Almost* a wish.

Jade had to admit that they weren't off to a very promising start. The night air was too quiet; there wasn't the faintest sound of a car coming. She was tired and worried and beginning to be very, very hungry.

Jade turned to look at her sisters.

"Well, where *is* she?"

"I don't know," Rowan said in her most doggedly gentle voice. "Be patient."

"Well, maybe we should scan for her."

"No," Rowan said. "Absolutely not. Remember what we decided."

"She's probably forgotten we were coming," Kestrel said. "I told you she was getting senile."

"Don't *say* things like that. It's not *polite,*" Rowan said, still gentle, but through her teeth.

Rowan was always gentle when she could manage it. She was nineteen, tall, slim, and stately. She had cinnamon-brown eyes and warm brown hair that cascaded down her back in waves.

Kestrel was seventeen and had hair the color of old gold sweeping back from her face like a bird's wings. Her eyes were amber and hawklike, and she was never gentle.

Jade was the youngest, just turned sixteen, and she didn't look like either of her sisters. She had white-blond hair that she used as a veil to hide behind, and green eyes. People said she looked serene, but she almost never felt serene. Usually she was either madly excited or madly anxious and confused.

Right now it was anxious. She was worried about her battered, half-century-old Morocco leather suitcase. She couldn't hear a thing from inside it.

"Hey, why don't you two go down the road a little way and see if she's coming?"

Her sisters looked back at her. There were few things that Rowan and Kestrel agreed on, but Jade was one of them. She could see that they were about to team up against her.

"Now what?" Kestrel said, her teeth showing just briefly.

And Rowan said, "You're up to something. What are you up to, Jade?"

Jade smoothed her thoughts and her face out and just looked at them artlessly. She hoped.

They stared back for a few minutes, then looked at each

other, giving up. "We're going to have to walk, you know," Kestrel said to Rowan.

"There are worse things than walking," Rowan said. She pushed a stray wisp of chestnut-colored hair off her forehead and looked around the bus station—which consisted of a three-sided, glass-walled cubicle, and the splintering wooden bench. "I wish there was a telephone."

"Well, there isn't. And it's twenty miles to Briar Creek," Kestrel said, golden eyes glinting with a kind of grim enjoyment. "We should probably leave our bags here."

Alarm tingled through Jade. "No, *no.* I've got all my—all my clothes in there. Come on, twenty miles isn't so far." With one hand she picked up her cat carrier—it was homemade, just boards and wires—and with the other she picked up the suitcase. She got quite a distance down the road before she heard the crunch of gravel behind her. They were following: Rowan sighing patiently, Kestrel chuckling softly, her hair shining like old gold in the starlight.

The one-lane road was dark and deserted. But not entirely silent—there were dozens of tiny night sounds, all adding up to one intricate, harmonizing night stillness. It would have been pleasant, except that Jade's suitcase seemed to get heavier with every step, and she was hungrier than she had ever been before. She knew better than to mention it to Rowan, but it made her feel confused and weak.

Just when she was beginning to think she would have to

put the suitcase down and rest, she heard a new sound.

It was a car, coming from behind them. The engine was so loud that it seemed to take a long time to get close to them, but when it passed, Jade saw that it was actually going very fast. Then there was a rattling of gravel and the car stopped. It backed up and Jade saw a boy looking through the window at her.

There was another boy in the passenger seat. Jade looked at them curiously.

They seemed to be about Rowan's age, and they were both deeply tanned. The one in the driver's seat had blond hair and looked as if he hadn't washed in a while. The other one had brown hair. He was wearing a vest with no shirt underneath. He had a toothpick in his mouth.

They both looked back at Jade, seeming just as curious as she was. Then the driver's window slid down. Jade was fascinated by how quickly it went.

"Need a ride?" the driver said, with an oddly bright smile. His teeth shone in contrast to his dingy face.

Jade looked at Rowan and Kestrel, who were just catching up. Kestrel said nothing, but looked at the car through narrow, heavy-lashed amber eyes. Rowan's brown eyes were very warm.

"We sure would," she said, smiling. Then, doubtfully, "But we're going to Burdock Farm. It may be out of your way. . . ."

"Oh, hey, I know that place. It's not far," the one in the vest said around his toothpick. "Anyway, anything for a lady," he said, with what seemed to be an attempt at gallantry. He opened his door and got out of the car. "One of you can sit up front, and I can sit in back with the other two. Lucky me, huh?" he said to the driver.

"Lucky you," the driver said, smiling largely again. He opened his door, too. "You go on and put that cat carrier in front, and the suitcases can go in the trunk," he said.

Rowan smiled at Jade, and Jade knew what she was thinking. *I wonder if everybody out here is so friendly?* They distributed their belongings and then piled in the car, Jade in the front with the driver, Rowan and Kestrel in the back on either side of the vested guy. A minute later they were flying down the road at what Jade found a delightful speed, gravel crunching beneath the tires.

"I'm Vic," the driver said.

"I'm Todd," the vested guy said.

Rowan said, "I'm Rowan, and this is Kestrel. That's Jade up there."

"You girls friends?"

"We're sisters," Jade said.

"You don't look like sisters."

"Everybody says that." Jade meant everybody they had met since they'd run away. Back home, everybody *knew* they were sisters, so nobody said it.

"What are you doing out here so late?" Vic asked. "It's not the place for nice girls."

"We're not nice girls," Kestrel explained absently.

"We're *trying* to be," Rowan said reprovingly through her teeth. To Vic, she said, "We were waiting for our great-aunt Opal to pick us up at the bus stop, but she didn't come. We're going to live at Burdock Farm."

"Old lady Burdock is your aunt?" Todd said, removing his toothpick. "That crazy old bat?" Vic turned around to look at him, and they both laughed and shook their heads.

Jade looked away from Vic. She stared down at the cat carrier, listening for the little squeaking noises that meant Tiggy was awake.

She felt just slightly . . . uneasy. She sensed something. Even though these guys seemed friendly, there was something beneath the surface. But she was too sleepy—and too light-headed from hunger—to figure out exactly what it was.

They seemed to drive a long time before Vic spoke again.

"You girls ever been to Oregon before?"

Jade blinked and murmured a negative.

"It's got some pretty lonely places," Vic said. "Out here, for example. Briar Creek was a gold rush town, but when the gold ran out and the railroad passed it by, it just died. Now the wilderness is taking it back."

His tone was significant, but Jade didn't understand what he was trying to convey.

"It does seem peaceful," Rowan said politely from the backseat.

Vic made a brief snorting sound. "Yeah, well, peaceful wasn't exactly what I meant. I meant, take this road. These farmhouses are miles apart, right? If you screamed, there wouldn't be anyone to hear you."

Jade blinked. What a strange thing to say.

Rowan, still politely making conversation, said, "Well, you and Todd would."

"I mean, nobody *else,*" Vic said, and Jade could feel his impatience. He had been driving more and more slowly. Now he pulled the car off to the side of the road and stopped. Parked.

"Nobody out *there* is going to hear," he clarified, turning around to look into the backseat. Jade looked, too, and saw Todd grinning, a wide bright grin with teeth clenched on his toothpick.

"That's right," Todd said. "You're out here alone with us, so maybe you'd better listen to us, huh?"

Jade saw that he was gripping Rowan's arm with one hand and Kestrel's wrist with the other.

Rowan was still looking polite and puzzled, but Kestrel looked at the car door on her side thoughtfully. Jade knew what she was looking for—a handle. There wasn't one.

"Too bad," Vic said. "This car's a real junkheap; you can't even open the back doors from inside."

He grabbed Jade's upper arm so hard she could feel pressure on the bone. "Now, you girls just be nice and nobody's going to get hurt."

CHAPTER 2

"You see, we're both lonely guys," Todd said from the back. "There aren't any girls our age around here, so we're lonely. And then when we come across three nice girls like you—well, we just naturally want to get to know you better. Understand?"

"So if you girls play along, we can all have fun," Vic put in.

"Fun—oh, no," Rowan said, dismayed. Jade knew she had caught part of Vic's thought and was trying very hard not to pry further. "Kestrel and Jade are much too young for anything like that. I'm sorry, but we have to say no."

"I won't do it even when I *am* old enough," Jade said. "But that isn't what these guys mean, anyway—they mean this." She projected some of the images she was getting from Vic into Rowan's mind.

"Oh, dear," Rowan said flatly. "Jade, you know we agreed not to spy on people like that."

Yeah, but look what they're thinking, Jade said soundlessly, figuring that if she had broken one rule, she might as well break them all.

"Now, look," Vic said in a tone that showed he knew he was losing control of the situation. He reached out and grabbed Jade's other arm, forcing her to face him. "We're not here to talk. See?" He gave her a little shake. Jade studied his features a moment, then turned her head to look inquiringly into the backseat.

Rowan's face was creamy-pale against her brown hair. Jade could feel that she was sad and disappointed. Kestrel's hair was dim gold and she was frowning.

Well? Kestrel said silently to Rowan.

Well? Jade said the same way. She wriggled as Vic tried to pull her closer. *Come on, Rowan, he's pinching me.*

I guess we don't have any choice, Rowan said.

Immediately Jade turned back to Vic. He was still trying to pull her, looking surprised that she didn't seem to be coming. Jade stopped resisting and let him drag her in close—and then smoothly detached one arm from his grip and slammed her hand upward. The heel of her hand made contact just under his chin. His teeth clicked and his head was knocked backward, exposing his throat.

Jade darted in and bit.

She was feeling guilty and excited. She wasn't used to doing it like this, to taking down prey that was awake and struggling instead of hypnotized and docile. But she knew her instincts were as good as any hunter who'd grown up stalking humans in alleys. It was part of her genetic programming to evaluate anything she saw in terms of "Is it food? Can I get it? What are its weaknesses?"

The only problem was that she shouldn't be enjoying this feeding, because it was exactly the opposite of what she and Rowan and Kestrel had come to Briar Creek to do.

She was tangentially aware of activity in the backseat. Rowan had lifted the arm Todd had been using to restrain her. On the other side Kestrel had done the same.

Todd was fighting, his voice thunderstruck. "Hey—hey, what are you—"

Rowan bit.

"What are you doing?"

Kestrel bit.

"What the freak are you doing? Who are you? What the freak are you?"

He thrashed wildly for a minute or so, and then subsided as Rowan and Kestrel mentally urged him into a trance.

It was only another minute or so before Rowan said, "That's enough."

Jade said, *Aw, Rowan . . .*

"That's *enough.* Tell him not to remember anything about this—and find out if he knows where Burdock Farm is."

Still feeding, Jade reached out with her mind, touching lightly with a tentacle of thought. Then she pulled back, her mouth closing as if in a kiss as it left Vic's skin. Vic was just a big rag doll at this point, and he flopped bonelessly against the steering wheel and the car door when she let him go.

"The farm's back that way—we have to go back to the fork in the road," she said. "It's weird," she added, puzzled. "He was thinking that he wouldn't get in trouble for attacking us because—because of something about Aunt Opal. I couldn't get what."

"Probably that she was crazy," Kestrel said unemotionally. "Todd was thinking that he wouldn't get in trouble because his dad's an Elder."

"They don't have Elders," Jade said, vaguely smug. "You mean a governor or a police officer or something."

Rowan was frowning, not looking at them. "All right," she said. "This was an emergency; we had to do it. But now we're going back to what we agreed."

"Until the next emergency," Kestrel said, smiling out the car window into the night.

To forestall Rowan, Jade said, "You think we should just leave them here?"

"Why not?" Kestrel said carelessly. "They'll wake up in a few hours."

Jade looked at Vic's neck. The two little wounds where her teeth had pierced him were already almost closed. By tomorrow they would be faint red marks like old bee stings.

Five minutes later they were on the road again with their

suitcases. This time, though, Jade was cheerful. The difference was food—she felt as full of blood as a tick, charged with energy and ready to skip up mountains. She swung the cat carrier and her suitcase alternately, and Tiggy growled.

It was wonderful being out like this, walking alone in the warm night air, with nobody to frown in disapproval. Wonderful to listen to the deer and rabbits and rats feeding in the meadows around her. Happiness bubbled up inside Jade. She'd never felt so free.

"It is nice, isn't it?" Rowan said softly, looking around as they reached the fork in the road. "It's the real world. And we have as much right to it as anybody else."

"I think it's the blood," Kestrel said. "Free-range humans are so much better than the kept ones. Why didn't our dear brother ever mention that?"

Ash, Jade thought, and felt a cold wind. She glanced behind her, not looking for a car but for something much more silent and deadly. She realized suddenly how fragile her bubble of happiness was.

"Are we going to get caught?" she asked Rowan. Reverting, in the space of one second, to a six-year-old turning to her big sister for help.

And Rowan, the best big sister in the world, said immediately and positively, *"No."*

"But if Ash figures it out—he's the only one who might realize—"

"We are not going to get caught," Rowan said. "Nobody will figure out that we're here."

Jade felt better. She put down her suitcase and held out a hand to Rowan, who took it. "Together forever," she said.

Kestrel, who'd been a few steps ahead, glanced over her shoulder. Then she came back and put her hand on theirs.

"Together forever."

Rowan said it solemnly; Kestrel said it with a quick narrowing of her yellow eyes. Jade said it with utter determination.

As they walked on, Jade felt buoyant and cheerful again, enjoying the velvet-dark night.

The road was just dirt here, not paved. They passed meadows and stands of Douglas fir. A farmhouse on the left, set back on a long driveway. And finally, dead ahead at the end of the road, another house.

"That's it," Rowan said. Jade recognized it, too, from the pictures Aunt Opal had sent them. It had two stories, a wraparound porch, and a steeply pitched roof with lots of gables. A cupola sprouted out of the rooftop, and there was a weather vane on the barn.

A real weather vane, Jade thought, stopping to stare. Her happiness flooded back full force. "I love it," she said solemnly.

Rowan and Kestrel had stopped, too, but their expressions were far from awed. Rowan looked a hairs-breadth away from horrified.

"It's a wreck," she gasped. "Look at that barn—the paint's completely gone. The pictures didn't show that."

"And the porch," Kestrel said helpfully. "It's falling to pieces. Might go any minute."

"The work," Rowan whispered. "The work it would take to fix this place up . . ."

"And the money," Kestrel said.

Jade gave them a cold look. "Why fix it? I like it. It's different." Rigid with superiority, she picked up her luggage and walked to the end of the road. There was a ramshackle, mostly fallen-down fence around the property, and a dangerous-looking gate. Beyond, on a weed-covered path, was a pile of white pickets—as if somebody had been planning to fix the fence but had never got around to it.

Jade put down the suitcase and cat carrier and pulled at the gate. To her surprise, it moved easily.

"See, it may not look good, but it still works—" She didn't get to finish the sentence properly. The gate fell on her.

"Well, it may not work, but it's still ours," she said as Rowan and Kestrel pulled it off her.

"No, it's Aunt Opal's," Kestrel said.

Rowan just smoothed her hair back and said, "Come on."

There was a board missing from the porch steps, and several boards gone from the porch itself. Jade limped around them with dignity. The gate had given her a good whack in the shin, and since it was wood, it still hurt. In fact, everything seemed to be made of wood here, which gave Jade a pleasantly alarmed feeling. Back home, wood was revered—and kept out of the way.

You have to be awfully careful to live in this kind of world, Jade thought. Or you're going to get hurt.

Rowan and Kestrel were knocking on the door, Rowan politely, with her knuckles, Kestrel loudly, with the side of her hand. There wasn't any answer.

"She doesn't seem to be here," Rowan said.

"She's decided she doesn't want us," Kestrel said, golden eyes gleaming.

"Maybe she went to the wrong bus station," Jade said.

"Oh—that's it. I bet that's it," Rowan said. "Poor old thing, she's waiting for us somewhere, and she's going to be thinking that we didn't show up."

"Sometimes you're not completely stupid," Kestrel informed Jade. High praise from Kestrel.

"Well, let's go in," Jade said, to conceal how pleased she was. "She'll come back here sometime."

"Human houses have locks," Rowan began, but this house wasn't locked. The doorknob turned in Jade's hand. The three of them stepped inside.

It was dark, even darker than the moonless night outside, but Jade's eyes adjusted in a few seconds.

"Hey, it's not bad," she said. They were in a shabby but handsome living room filled with huge, ponderous furniture. Wood furniture, of course—dark and highly polished. The tables were topped with marble.

Rowan found a light switch, and suddenly the room was

too bright. Blinking, Jade saw that the walls were pale apple green, with fancy woodwork and moldings in a darker shade of the same green. It made Jade feel oddly peaceful. And anchored, somehow, as if she belonged here. Maybe it was all the heavy furniture.

She looked at Rowan, who was looking around, tall graceful body slowly relaxing.

Rowan smiled and met her eyes. She nodded, once. "Yes."

Jade basked for a moment in the glory of having been right twice in five minutes—and then she remembered her suitcase.

"Let's see what the rest of the place is like," she said hastily. "I'll take the upstairs; you guys look around here."

"You just want the best bedroom," Kestrel said.

Jade ignored her, hurrying up a wide, carpeted flight of stairs. There were lots of bedrooms, and each one had lots of room. She didn't want the best, though, just the farthest away.

At the very end of the hall was a room painted sea-blue. Jade slammed the door behind her and put her suitcase on the bed. Holding her breath, she opened the suitcase.

Oh. Oh, *no.* Oh, *no* . . .

Three minutes later she heard the click of the door behind her, but didn't care enough to turn.

"What are you *doing*?" Kestrel's voice said.

Jade looked up from her frantic efforts to resuscitate the two kittens she held. "They're *dead*!" she wailed.

"Well, what did you expect? They need to breathe, idiot. How did you expect them to make it through two days of traveling?"

Jade sniffled.

"Rowan told you that you could take only one."

Jade sniffled harder and glared. "I *know.* That's why I put these two in the suitcase." She hiccuped. "At least Tiggy's all right." She dropped to her knees and peered in the cat carrier to make sure he *was* all right. His ears were laid back, his golden eyes gleaming out of a mass of black fur. He hissed, and Jade sat up. He was fine.

"For five dollars I'll take care of the dead ones," Kestrel said.

"No!" Jade jumped up and moved protectively in front of them, fingers clawed.

"Not like *that,*" Kestrel said, offended. "I don't eat carrion. Look, if you don't get rid of them somehow, Rowan's going to find out. For God's sake, girl, you're a vampire," she added as Jade cradled the limp bodies to her chest. "Act like one."

"I want to bury them," Jade said. "They should have a funeral."

Kestrel rolled her eyes and left. Jade wrapped the small corpses in her jacket and tiptoed out after her.

A shovel, she thought. Now, where would that be?

Keeping her ears open for Rowan, she sidled around the first floor. All the rooms looked like the living room: imposing and in a state of genteel decay. The kitchen was huge. It had an open fireplace and a shed off the back door for washing laundry. It also had a door to the cellar.

Jade made her way down the steps cautiously. She couldn't turn on a light because she needed both hands for the kittens. And, because of the kittens, she couldn't see her feet. She had to feel with her toe for the next step.

At the bottom of the stairs her toe found something yielding, slightly resilient. It was blocking her path.

Slowly Jade craned her neck over the bundle of jacket and looked down.

It was dim here. She herself was blocking the light that filtered down from the kitchen. But she could make out what looked like a pile of old clothes. A lumpy pile.

Jade was getting a very, very bad feeling.

She nudged the pile of clothes with one toe. It moved slightly. Jade took a deep breath and nudged it hard.

It was all one piece. It rolled over. Jade looked down, breathed quickly for a moment, and screamed.

A good, shrill, attention-getting scream. She added a nonverbal thought, the telepathic equivalent of a siren.

Rowan! Kestrel! You guys get down here!

Twenty seconds later the cellar light went on and Rowan and Kestrel came clattering down the stairs.

"I have told you and *told* you," Rowan was saying through her teeth. "We don't use our—" She stopped, staring.

"I think it's Aunt Opal," Jade said.

CHAPTER 3

She's not looking so good," Kestrel said, peering over Rowan's shoulder.

Rowan said, "Oh, *dear,*" and sat down.

Great-aunt Opal was a mummy. Her skin was like leather: yellow-brown, hard, and smooth. Almost shiny. And the skin was all there was to her, just a leathery frame stretched over bones. She didn't have any hair. Her eye sockets were dark holes with dry tissue inside. Her nose was collapsed.

"Poor auntie," Rowan said. Her own brown eyes were wet.

"We're going to look like that when we die," Kestrel said musingly.

Jade stamped her foot. "No, *look,* you guys! You're both missing it completely. Look at *that*!" She swung a wild toe at the mummy's midsection. There, protruding from the blue-flowered housedress and the leathery skin, was a gigantic splinter of wood. It was almost as long as an arrow, thick at the base and tapered where it disappeared into Aunt Opal's chest. Flakes of white paint still clung to one side.

Several other pickets were lying on the cellar floor.

"Poor old thing," Rowan said. "She must have been carrying them when she fell."

Jade looked at Kestrel. Kestrel looked back with exasperated golden eyes. There were few things they agreed on, but Rowan was one of them.

"Rowan," Kestrel said distinctly, "she was *staked.*"

"Oh, no."

"Oh, yes," Jade said. "Somebody killed her. And somebody who knew she was a vampire."

Rowan was shaking her head. "But who would know that?"

"Well . . ." Jade thought. "Another vampire."

"Or a vampire *hunter*," Kestrel said.

Rowan looked up, shocked. "Those aren't real. They're just stories to frighten kids—aren't they?"

Kestrel shrugged, but her golden eyes were dark.

Jade shifted uneasily. The freedom she'd felt on the road, the peace in the living room—and now *this.* Suddenly she felt empty and isolated.

Rowan sat down on the stairs, looking too tired and preoccupied to push back the lock of hair plastered to her forehead. "Maybe I shouldn't have brought you here," she said softly. "Maybe it's worse here." She didn't say it, but

Jade could sense her next thought. *Maybe we should go back.*

"*Nothing* could be worse," Jade said fiercely. "And I'd *die* before I'd go back." She meant it. Back to waiting on every man in sight? Back to arranged marriages and endless restrictions? Back to all those disapproving faces, so quick to condemn anything different, anything that wasn't done the way it had been done four hundred years ago?

"We *can't* go back," she said.

"No, we can't," Kestrel said dryly. "Literally. Unless we want to end up like Great-aunt Opal. Or"—she paused significantly—"like Great-uncle Hodge."

Rowan looked up. "Don't even say that!"

Jade's stomach felt like a clenched fist. "They wouldn't," she said, shoving back at the memory that was trying to emerge. "Not to their own grandkids. Not to us."

"The point," Kestrel said, "is that we can't go back, so we have to go forward. We've got to figure out what we're going to do here without Aunt Opal to help us—especially if there's a vampire hunter around. But first, what are we going to do with *that*?" She nodded toward the body.

Rowan just shook her head helplessly. She looked around the cellar as if she might find an answer in a corner. Her gaze fell on Jade. It stopped there, and Jade could see the sisterly radar system turn on.

"Jade. What's that in your jacket?"

Jade was too wrung-out to lie. She opened the jacket

and showed Rowan the kittens. "I didn't know my suitcase would kill them."

Rowan looked too wrung-out to be angry. She glanced heavenward, sighing. Then, looking back at Jade sharply: "But why were you bringing them down *here*?"

"I wasn't. I was just looking for a shovel. I was going to bury them in the backyard."

There was a pause. Jade looked at her sisters and they looked at each other. Then all three of them looked at the kittens.

Then they looked at Great-aunt Opal.

Mary-Lynnette was crying.

It was a beautiful night, a perfect night. An inversion layer was keeping the air overhead still and warm, and the seeing was excellent. There was very little light pollution and no direct light. The Victorian farmhouse just below Mary-Lynnette's hill was mostly dark. Mrs. Burdock was always very considerate about that.

Above, the Milky Way cut diagonally across the sky like a river. To the south, where Mary-Lynnette had just directed her telescope, was the constellation Sagittarius, which always looked more like a teapot than like an archer to her. And just above the spout of the teapot was a faintly pink patch of what looked like steam.

It wasn't steam. It was clouds of stars. A star factory called the Lagoon Nebula. The dust and gas of dead stars was being recycled into hot young stars, just being born.

It was four thousand and five hundred light-years away. And she was looking at it, right this minute. A seventeen-year-old kid with a second-hand Newtonian reflector telescope was watching the light of stars being born.

Sometimes she was filled with so much awe and—and—and—and *longing*—that she thought she might break to pieces.

Since there was nobody else around, she could let the tears roll down her cheeks without pretending it was an allergy. After a while she had to sit back and wipe her nose and eyes on the shoulder of her T-shirt.

Oh, come on, give it a rest now, she told herself. You're *crazy*, you know.

She wished she hadn't thought of Jeremy earlier. Because now, for some reason, she kept picturing him the way he'd looked that night when he came to watch the eclipse with her. His level brown eyes had held a spark of excitement, as if he really cared about what he was seeing. As if, for that moment, anyway, he understood.

I have been one acquainted with the night, a maudlin little voice inside her chanted romantically, trying to get her to cry again.

Yeah, right, Mary-Lynnette told the voice cynically. She reached for the bag of Cheetos she kept under her lawn chair.

It was impossible to feel romantic and overwhelmed by grandeur while eating Cheetos.

Saturn next, she thought, and wiped sticky orange crumbs off her fingers. It was a good night for Saturn because its rings were just passing through their edgewise position.

She had to hurry because the moon was rising at 11:16. But before she turned her telescope toward Saturn, she took one last look at the Lagoon. Actually just to the east of the Lagoon, trying to make out the open cluster of fainter stars she knew was there.

She couldn't see it. Her eyes just weren't good enough. If she had a bigger telescope—if she lived in Chile where the air was dry—if she could get above the earth's atmosphere . . . then she might have a chance. But for now . . . she was limited by the human eye. Human pupils just didn't open farther than 9 millimeters.

Nothing to be done about *that.*

She was just centering Saturn in the field of view when a light went on behind the farmhouse below. Not a little porch light. A barnyard vapor lamp. It illuminated the back property of the house like a searchlight.

Mary-Lynnette sat back, annoyed. It didn't really matter—she could see Saturn anyway, see the rings that tonight were just a delicate silver line cutting across the center of the planet. But it was strange. Mrs. Burdock never turned the back light on at night.

The girls, Mary-Lynnette thought. The nieces. They must have gotten there and she must be giving them a tour. Absently she reached for her binoculars. She was curious.

They were good binoculars, Celestron Ultimas, sleek and lightweight. She used them for looking at everything from deep sky objects to the craters on the moon. Right now, they magnified the back of Mrs. Burdock's house ten times.

She didn't see Mrs. Burdock, though. She could see the garden. She could see the shed and the fenced-in area where Mrs. Burdock kept her goats. And she could see three girls, all well illuminated by the vapor lamp. One had brown hair, one had golden hair, and one had hair the color of Jupiter's rings. That silvery. Like starlight. They were carrying something wrapped in plastic between them. Black plastic. Hefty garbage bags, if Mary-Lynnette wasn't mistaken.

Now, what on earth were they doing with that?

Burying it.

The short one with the silvery hair had a shovel. She was a good little digger, too. In a few minutes she had rooted up most of Mrs. Burdock's irises. Then the medium-sized one with the golden hair took a turn, and last of all the tall one with the brown hair.

Then they picked up the garbage-bagged object—even though it was probably over five feet long, it seemed very light—and put it in the hole they'd just made.

They began to shovel dirt back into the hole.

No, Mary-Lynnette told herself. No, don't be ridiculous. Don't be *insane.* There's some mundane, perfectly commonplace explanation for this.

The problem was, she couldn't think of any.

No, no, no. This is not *Rear Window*, we are not in the Twilight Zone. They're just burying—something. Some sort of . . . ordinary . . .

What else besides a dead body was five-feet-and-some-odd-inches long, rigid, and needed to be wrapped in garbage bags before burial?

And, Mary-Lynnette thought, feeling a rush of adrenaline that made her heart beat hard. And. *And* . . .

Where was Mrs. Burdock?

The adrenaline was tingling painfully in her palms and feet. It made her feel out of control, which she hated. Her hands were shaking so badly she had to lower the binoculars.

Mrs. B.'s okay. She's all right. Things like this don't *happen* in real life.

What would Nancy Drew do?

Suddenly, in the middle of her panic, Mary-Lynnette felt a tiny giggle try to escape like a burp. Nancy Drew, of course, would hike right down there and investigate. She'd eavesdrop on the girls from behind a bush and then dig up the garden once they went back inside the house.

But things like that *didn't* happen. Mary-Lynnette couldn't even imagine trying to dig up a neighbor's garden in the dead of night. She would get caught and it would be a humiliating farce. Mrs. Burdock would walk out of the house alive and alarmed, and Mary-Lynnette would *die* of embarrassment trying to explain.

In a book that might be amusing. In real life—she didn't even want to think about it.

One good thing, it made her realize how absurd her paranoia was. Deep down, she obviously knew Mrs. B. was just fine. Otherwise, she wouldn't be sitting here; she'd be calling the police, like any sensible person.

Somehow, though, she suddenly felt tired. Not up to more starwatching. She checked her watch by the ruby glow of a red-filtered flashlight. Almost eleven—well, it was all over in sixteen minutes anyway. When the moon rose it would bleach out the sky.

But before she broke down her telescope for the trip back, she picked up the binoculars again. Just one last look.

The garden was empty. A rectangle of fresh dark soil showed where it had been violated. Even as Mary-Lynnette watched, the vapor lamp went out.

It wouldn't do any harm to go over there tomorrow, Mary-Lynnette thought. Actually, I was going to, anyway. I should welcome those girls to the neighborhood. I should return those pruning shears Dad borrowed and the knife Mrs. B. gave me to get my gas cap off. And of course I'll see Mrs. B. there, and then I'll know everything's okay.

• • •

Ash reached the top of the winding road and stopped to admire the blazing point of light in the south. You really could see more from these isolated country towns. From here Jupiter, the king of the planets, looked like a UFO.

"Where have you been?" a voice nearby said. "I've been waiting for you for hours."

Ash answered without turning around. "Where have *I* been? Where have *you* been? We were supposed to meet on *that* hill, Quinn." Hands in his pockets, he pointed with an elbow.

"Wrong. It was this hill and I've been sitting right here waiting for you the entire time. But forget it. Are they here or aren't they?"

Ash turned and walked unhurriedly to the open convertible that was parked just beside the road, its lights off. He leaned one elbow on the door, looking down. "They're here. I told you they would be. It was the only place for them to go."

"All three of them?"

"Of course, all three of them. My sisters always stick together."

Quinn's lip curled. "Lamia are so wonderfully family oriented."

"And made vampires are so wonderfully . . . short," Ash said serenely, looking at the sky again.

Quinn gave him a look like black ice. His small compact

body was utterly still inside the car. "Well now, I never got to finish growing, did I?" he said very softly. "One of your ancestors took care of that."

Ash boosted himself to sit on the hood of the car, long legs dangling. "I think I may stop aging this year myself," he said blandly, still looking down the slope. "Eighteen's not such a bad age."

"Maybe not if you have a choice," Quinn said, his voice still as soft as dead leaves falling. "Try being eighteen for four centuries—with no end in sight."

Ash turned to smile at him again. "Sorry. On my family's behalf."

"And I'm sorry for your family. The Redferns have been having a little trouble lately, haven't they? Let's see if I've got it right. First your uncle Hodge breaks Night World law and is appropriately punished—"

"My great-uncle by marriage," Ash interrupted in polite tones, holding one finger up. "He was a Burdock, not a Redfern. And that was over ten years ago."

"And then your aunt Opal—"

"My *great-aunt* Opal—"

"Disappears completely. Breaks off all contact with the Night World. Apparently because she prefers living in the middle of nowhere with humans."

Ash shrugged, eyes fixed on the southern horizon. "It must be good hunting in the middle of nowhere with humans. No competition. And no Night World enforcement—no Elders putting a limit on how many you can bag."

"And no supervision," Quinn said sourly. "It doesn't matter so much that *she's* been living here, but she's obviously been encouraging your sisters to join her. You should have informed on them when you found out they were writing to each other secretly."

Ash shrugged, uncomfortable. "It wasn't against the law. I didn't know what they had in mind."

"It's not just them," Quinn said in his disturbingly soft voice. "You know there are rumors about that cousin of yours—James Rasmussen. People are saying that he fell in love with a human girl. That she was dying and he decided to change her without permission. . . ."

Ash slid off the hood and straightened. "I never listen to rumors," he said, briskly and untruthfully. "Besides, that's not the problem right now, is it?"

"No. The problem is your sisters and the mess they're in. And whether you can really do what's necessary to clean it up."

"Don't worry, Quinn. I can handle it."

"But I *do* worry, Ash. I don't know how I let you talk me into this."

"You didn't. You lost that game of poker."

"And you cheated." Quinn was looking off into a middle distance, his dark eyes narrowed, his mouth a straight line. "I still think we should tell the Elders," he said abruptly. "It's the only way to guarantee a really *thorough* investigation."

"I don't see why it needs to be so thorough. They've only been here a few hours."

"Your sisters have only been here a few hours. Your aunt has been here—how long? Ten years?"

"What have you got against my aunt, Quinn?"

"Her husband was a traitor. *She's* a traitor now for encouraging those girls to run away. And who knows what she's been doing here in the last ten years? Who knows how many humans she's told about the Night World?"

Ash shrugged, examining his nails. "Maybe she hasn't told any."

"And maybe she's told the whole town."

"Quinn," Ash said patiently, speaking as if to a very young child, "if my aunt has broken the laws of the Night World, she has to die. For the family honor. Any blotch on that reflects on *me*."

"That's one thing I can count on," Quinn said half under his breath. "Your self-interest. You always look after Number One, don't you?"

"Doesn't everybody?"

"Not everybody is quite so blatant about it." There was a pause, then Quinn said, "And what about your sisters?"

"What about them?"

"Can you kill them if it's necessary?"

Ash didn't blink. "Of course. If it's necessary. For the family honor."

"If they've let something slip about the Night World—"

"They're not stupid."

"They're innocent. They might get tricked. That's what happens when you live on an island completely isolated from normal humans. You never learn how cunning vermin can be."

"Well, *we* know how cunning they can be," Ash said, smiling. "And what to do about them."

For the first time Quinn himself smiled, a charming, almost dreamy smile. "Yes, I know your views on that. All right. I'll leave you here to take care of it. I don't need to tell you to check out every human those girls have had contact with. Do a good job and maybe you can save your family honor."

"Not to mention the embarrassment of a public trial."

"I'll come back in a week. And if you haven't got things under control, I go to the Elders. I don't mean your Redfern family Elders, either. I'm taking it all the way up to the joint Council."

"Oh, fine," Ash said. "You know, you really ought to get a hobby, Quinn. Go hunting yourself. You're too repressed."

Quinn ignored that and said shortly, "Do you know where to start?"

"Sure. The girls are right . . . down . . . there." Ash turned east. With one eye shut, he zeroed in with his finger on a patch of light in the valley below. "At Burdock Farm. I'll check things out in town, then I'll go look up the nearest vermin."

Chapter 4

What a difference a day made.

Somehow, in the hot, hazy August sunlight the next morning, Mary-Lynnette couldn't get serious about checking on whether Mrs. Burdock was dead. It was just too ridiculous. Besides, she had a lot to do—school started in just over two weeks. At the beginning of June she had been sure summer would last forever, sure that she would *never* say, "Wow, this summer has gone by so fast." And now here she stood in mid-August, and she was saying, "Wow, it's gone by so fast."

I need clothes, Mary-Lynnette thought. And a new backpack, and notebooks, and some of those little purple felt-tip pens. And I need to make Mark get all those things, too, because he won't do it by himself and Claudine will never make him.

Claudine was their stepmother. She was Belgian and very pretty, with curly dark hair and sparkling dark eyes. She was only ten years older than Mary-Lynnette, and she looked even younger. She'd been the family's housecleaning helper when Mary-Lynnette's mom first got sick five years ago. Mary-Lynnette liked her, but she was hopeless as a substitute mother, and Mary-Lynnette usually ended up taking charge of Mark.

So I don't have time to go over to Mrs. B.'s.

She spent the day shopping. It wasn't until after dinner that she thought about Mrs. Burdock again.

She was helping to clear dishes out of the family room, where dinner was traditionally eaten in front of the TV, when her father said, "I heard something today about Todd Akers and Vic Kimble."

"Those losers," Mark muttered.

Mary-Lynnette said, "What?"

"They had some kind of accident over on Chiloquin Road—over between Hazel Green Creek and Beavercreek."

"A car accident?" Mary-Lynnette said.

"Well, this is the thing," her father said. "Apparently there wasn't any damage to their car, but they both *thought* they'd been in an accident. They showed up at home after midnight and said that something had happened to them out there—but they didn't know what. They were missing a few hours." He looked at Mark and Mary-Lynnette. "How about that, guys?"

"It's the UFOs!" Mark shouted immediately, dropping into discus-throwing position and wiggling his plate.

"UFOs are a crock," Mary-Lynnette said. "Do you know how

far the little green men would have to travel—and there's no such *thing* as warp speed. Why do people have to make things up when the universe is just—just *blazing* with incredible things that are *real*—" She stopped. Her family was looking at her oddly.

"Actually Todd and Vic probably just got smashed," she said, and put her plate and glass in the sink. Her father grimaced slightly. Claudine pursed her lips. Mark grinned.

"In a very real and literal sense," he said. "We hope."

It was as Mary-Lynnette was walking back to the family room that a thought struck her.

Chiloquin Road was right off Kahneta, the road her own house was on. The road Mrs. B.'s house was on. It was only two miles from Burdock Farm to Chiloquin.

There couldn't be any connection. Unless the girls were burying the little green man who'd abducted Vic and Todd.

But it bothered her. Two really strange things happening in the same night, in the same area. In a tiny, sleepy area that never saw any kind of excitement.

I know, I'll call Mrs. B. And she'll be fine, and that'll prove everything's okay, and I'll be able to laugh about all this.

But nobody answered at the Burdock house. The phone rang and rang. Nobody picked it up and the answering machine never came on. Mary-Lynnette hung up feeling grim but oddly calm. She knew what she had to do now.

She snagged Mark as he was going up the stairs.

"I need to talk to you."

"Look, if this is about your Walkman—"

"Huh? It's about something we have to do tonight." Mary-Lynnette looked at him. "What about my Walkman?"

"Uh, nothing. Nothing at all."

Mary-Lynnette groaned but let it go. "Listen, I need you to help me out. Last night I saw something weird when I was on the hill. . . ." She explained as succinctly as possible. "And now more weird stuff with Todd and Vic," she said.

Mark was shaking his head, looking at her in something like pity. "Mare, Mare," he said kindly. "You really are crazy, you know."

"Yes," Mary-Lynnette said. "It doesn't matter. I'm still going over there tonight."

"To do *what*?"

"To check things out. I just want to *see* Mrs. B. If I can talk to her, I'll feel better. And if I can find out what's buried in that garden, I'll feel a whole *lot* better."

"Maybe they were burying Sasquatch. That government study in the Klamaths never did find him, you know."

"Mark, you owe me for the Walkman. For whatever happened to the Walkman."

"Uh . . ." Mark sighed, then muttered resignedly. "Okay, I owe you. But I'm telling you right now, I'm not going to talk to those girls."

"You don't have to talk to them. You don't even have to see them. There's something else I want you to do."

• • •

The sun was just setting. They'd walked this road a hundred times to get to Mary-Lynnette's hill—the only difference tonight was that Mark was carrying a pair of pruning shears and Mary-Lynnette had pulled the Rubylith filter off her flashlight.

"You don't *really* think they offed the old lady."

"No," Mary-Lynnette said candidly. "I just want to put the world back where it belongs."

"You want *what*?"

"You know how you have a view of the way the world is, but every so often you wonder, 'Oh, my God, what if it's really *different*?' Like, 'What if I'm really adopted and the people I think are my parents aren't my parents at all?' And if it were true, it would change everything, and for a minute you don't know what's real. Well, that's how I feel right now, and I want to get rid of it. I want my old world back."

"You know what's scary?" Mark said. "I think I understand."

By the time they got to Burdock Farm, it was full dark. Ahead of them, in the west, the star Arcturus seemed to hang over the farmhouse, glittering faintly red.

Mary-Lynnette didn't bother trying to deal with the rickety gate. She went to the place behind the blackberry bushes where the picket fence had fallen flat.

The farmhouse was like her own family's, but with lots of Victorian-style gingerbread added. Mary-Lynnette thought the spindles and scallops and fretwork gave it a whimsical air—eccentric, like Mrs. Burdock. Just now, as she was looking at one of the second-story windows, the shadow of a moving figure fell on the roller blind.

Good, Mary-Lynnette thought. At least I know somebody's home.

Mark began hanging back as they walked down the weedy path to the house.

"You said I could hide."

"Okay. Right. Look, why don't you take those shears and sort of go around back—"

"And look at the Sasquatch grave while I'm there? Maybe do a little digging? I don't *think* so."

"Fine," Mary-Lynnette said calmly. "Then hide somewhere out here and hope they don't see you when they come to the door. At least with the shears you have an excuse to be in the back."

Mark threw her a bitter glance and she knew she'd won. As he started off, Mary-Lynnette said suddenly, "Mark, be careful."

Mark just waved a dismissive hand at her without turning around.

When he was out of sight, Mary-Lynnette knocked on the front door. Then she rang the doorbell—it wasn't a button but an actual bellpull. She could hear chimes inside, but nobody answered.

She knocked and rang with greater authority. Every minute she kept expecting the door to open to reveal Mrs. B., petite, gravelly-voiced, blue-haired, dressed in an old cotton housedress. But it didn't happen. Nobody came.

Mary-Lynnette stopped being polite and began knocking with one hand and ringing with the other. It was somewhere in the middle of this frenzy of knocks and rings that she realized she was frightened.

Really frightened. Her world view was wobbling. Mrs. Burdock hardly ever left the house. She always answered the door. And Mary-Lynnette had seen with her own eyes that *somebody* was home here.

So why weren't they answering?

Mary-Lynnette's heart was beating very hard. She had an uncomfortable falling sensation in her stomach.

I should get out of here and call Sheriff Akers. It's his *job* to know what to do about things like this. But it was hard to work up any feeling of confidence in Todd's father. She took her alarm and frustration out on the door.

Which opened. Suddenly. Mary-Lynnette's fist hit air and for an instant she felt sheer panic, fear of the unknown.

"What can I do for you?"

The voice was soft and beautifully modulated. The girl was just plain beautiful. What Mary-Lynnette hadn't been able to see from the top of her hill was that the brown hair was aglow with rich chestnut highlights, the features were classically molded, the tall figure was graceful and willowy.

"You're Rowan," she said.

"How did you know?"

You couldn't be anything else; I've never seen anybody who looked so much like a tree spirit. "Your aunt told me about you. I'm Mary-Lynnette Carter; I live just up Kahneta Road. You probably saw my house on your way here."

Rowan looked noncommittal. She had such a sweet, grave face—and skin that looked like white orchid petals, Mary-Lynnette thought abstractedly. She said, "So, I just wanted to welcome you to the neighborhood, say hello, see if there's anything you need."

Rowan looked less grave; she almost smiled and her brown eyes grew warm. "How nice of you. Really. I almost wish we did need something . . . but actually we're fine."

Mary-Lynnette realized that, with the utmost civility and good manners, Rowan was winding up the conversation. Hastily she threw a new subject into the pool. "There are three of you girls, right? Are you going to school here?"

"My sisters are."

"That's great. I can help show them around. I'll be a senior this year." Another subject, quick, Mary-Lynnette thought. "So, how do you like Briar Creek? It's probably quieter than you're used to."

"Oh, it was pretty quiet where we came from," Rowan said. "But we love it here; it's such a wonderful place. The trees, the little animals . . ." She broke off.

"Yeah, those cute little animals," Mary-Lynnette said. Get to the *point*, her inner voices were telling her. Her tongue and the roof of her mouth felt like Velcro. Finally she blurted, "So—so, um, how is your aunt right now?"

"She's—fine."

That instant's hesitation was all Mary-Lynnette needed. Her old suspicions, her old panic, surged up immediately. Making her feel bright and cold, like a knife made of ice.

She found herself saying in a confident, almost chirpy voice, "Well, could I just talk to her for a minute? Would you mind? It's just that I have something sort of important to tell her. . . ." She made a move as if to step over the threshold.

Rowan kept on blocking the door. "Oh, I'm so sorry. But—well, that's not really possible right now."

"Oh, is it one of her headaches? I've seen her in bed before." Mary-Lynnette gave a little tinkly laugh.

"No, it's not a headache." Rowan spoke gently, deliberately. "The truth is that she's gone for a few days."

"Gone?"

"I know." Rowan made a little grimace acknowledging that this was odd. "She just decided to take a few days off. A little vacation."

"But—gosh, with you girls just getting here . . ." Mary-Lynnette's voice was brittle.

"Well, you see, she knew we'd take care of the house for her. That's why she waited until we came."

"But—gosh," Mary-Lynnette said again. She felt a spasm in her throat. "Where—just where did she go?"

"Up north, somewhere on the coast. I'm not sure of the name of the town."

"But . . ." Mary-Lynnette's voice trailed off. Back off, her inner voices warned. *Now* was the time to be polite, to be cautious. Pushing it meant showing this girl that Mary-Lynnette knew something was wrong with this story. And since something *was* wrong, this girl might be dangerous. . . .

It was hard to believe that while looking at Rowan's sweet, grave face. She didn't *look* dangerous. But then Mary-Lynnette noticed something else. Rowan was barefoot. Her feet were as creamy-pale as the rest of her, but sinewy. Something about them, the way they were placed or the clean definition of the toes, made Mary-Lynnette think of those feet running. Of savage, primal speed.

When she looked up, there was another girl walking up behind Rowan. The one with dark golden hair. Her skin was milky instead of blossomy, and her eyes were yellow.

"This is Kestrel," Rowan said.

"Yes," Mary-Lynnette said. She realized she was staring. And realized, the moment after that, that she was scared. *Everything* about Kestrel made her think of savage, primal movement. The girl walked as if she were flying.

"What's going on?" Kestrel said.

"This is Mary-Lynnette," Rowan said, her voice still pleasant. "She lives down the road. She came to see Aunt Opal."

"Really just to see if you needed anything," Mary-Lynnette

interjected quickly. "We're sort of your only neighbors." Strategy change, she was thinking. About-face. Looking at Kestrel, she believed in danger. Now all she wanted was to keep these girls from guessing what she knew.

"You're a friend of Aunt Opal's?" Kestrel asked silkily. Her yellow eyes swept Mary-Lynnette, first up, then down.

"Yeah, I come over sometimes, help her with the"—oh, God, don't say gardening—"goats. Um, I guess she told you that they need to be milked every twelve hours."

Rowan's expression changed fractionally. Mary-Lynnette's heart gave a violent thud. Mrs. B. would never, *ever* leave without giving instructions about the goats.

"Of course she told us," Rowan said smoothly, just an instant too late.

Mary-Lynnette's palms were sweating. Kestrel hadn't taken that keen, dispassionate, unblinking gaze off her for a moment. Like the proverbial bird of prey staring down the proverbial rabbit. "Well, it's getting late and I bet you guys have things to do. I should let you go."

Rowan and Kestrel looked at each other. Then they both looked at Mary-Lynnette, cinnamon-brown eyes and golden eyes fixed intently on her face. Mary-Lynnette had the falling feeling in her stomach again.

"Oh, don't go yet," Kestrel said silkily. "Why don't you come inside?"

CHAPTER 5

Mark was still muttering as he rounded the back corner of the house. What was he even *doing* here?

It wasn't easy to get into the garden area from outside. He had to bushwhack through the overgrown rhododendron bushes and blackberry canes that formed a dense hedge all around it. And even when he emerged from a tunnel of leathery green leaves, the scene in front of him didn't immediately register. His momentum kept him going for a few steps before his brain caught up.

Hey, wait. There's a *girl* here.

A pretty girl. An *extremely* pretty girl. He could see her clearly by the back porch light. She had hip-length white-blond hair, the color that normally only preschoolers have, and it was as fine as a child's hair, too, whipping around her like pale silk when she moved. She was smallish. Little bones. Her hands and feet were delicate.

She was wearing what looked like an old-fashioned nightshirt and dancing to what sounded like a rent-to-own commercial. There was a battered clock radio on the porch steps. There was also a black kitten that took one look at Mark and darted away into the shadows.

"*Baaad* cred-it, *nooo* cred-it, *dooon't* wor-ry, *weee'll* take you. . . ." the radio warbled. The girl danced with her arms above her head—light as thistledown, Mark thought, staring in astonishment. Really, actually that light, and so what if it was a cliché?

As the commercial ended and a country western song began, she did a twirl and saw him. She stopped, frozen, arms still above her head, wrists crossed. Her eyes got big and her mouth sagged open.

She's scared, Mark thought. Of me. The girl didn't look graceful now; she was scrambling to seize the clock radio, fumbling with it, shaking it. Trying to find an off switch, Mark realized. Her desperation was contagious. Before he thought, Mark dropped the pruning shears and swooped in to grab the radio from her. He twisted the top dial, cutting the song short. Then he stared at the girl, who stared back with wide silvery-green eyes. They were both breathing quickly, as if they'd just disarmed a bomb.

"Hey, I hate country western, too," Mark said after a minute, shrugging.

He'd never talked to a girl this way before. But then he'd

never had a girl look scared of him before. And *so* scared—he imagined he could see her heart beating in the pale blue veins beneath the translucent skin of her throat.

Then, suddenly, she stopped looking terrified. She bit her lip and chortled. Then, still grinning, she blinked and sniffed.

"I forgot," she said, dabbing at the corner of her eye. "You don't have the same rules we do."

"Rules about country western music?" Mark hazarded. He liked her voice. It was ordinary, not celestial. It made her seem more human.

"Rules about *any* music from outside," she said. "And any TV, too."

Outside what? Mark thought. He said, "Uh, hi. I'm Mark Carter."

"I'm Jade Redfern."

"You're one of Mrs. Burdock's nieces."

"Yes. We just came last night. We're going to live here."

Mark snorted and muttered, "You have my condolences."

"Condolences? Why?" Jade cast a darting glance around the garden.

"Because living in Briar Creek is just slightly more exciting than living in a cemetery."

She gave him a long, fascinated look. "You've . . . lived in a cemetery?"

He gave *her* a long look. "Uh, actually, I just meant it's boring here."

"Oh." She thought, then smiled. "Well, it's interesting to us," she said. "It's different from where we come from."

"And just where *do* you come from?"

"An island. It's sort of near . . ." She considered. "The state of Maine."

"'The state of Maine.'"

"Yeah."

"Does this island have a name?"

She stared at him with wide green eyes. "Well, I can't tell you *that.*"

"Uh—okay." Was she making fun of him? But there was nothing like mockery or sly teasing in her face. She looked mysterious . . . and innocent. Maybe she had some kind of mental problem. The kids at Dewitt High School would have a field day with that. They weren't very tolerant of differences.

"Look," he said abruptly. "If there's ever anything I can do for you—you know, if you ever get in trouble or something—then just tell me. Okay?"

She tilted her head sideways. Her eyelashes actually cast shadows in the porch light, but her expression wasn't coy. It was straightforward and assessing, and she was looking him over carefully, as if she needed to figure him out. She took her time doing it. Then she smiled, making little dimples in her cheeks, and Mark's heart jumped unexpectedly.

"Okay," she said softly. "Mark. You're not silly, even though you're a boy. You're a good guy, aren't you?"

"Well . . ." Mark had never been called upon to be a good guy, not in the TV sense. He wasn't sure how he'd measure up if he were. "I, um, hope I am."

Jade was looking at him steadily. "You know, I just decided. I'm going to like it here." She smiled again, and Mark found it hard to breathe—and then her expression changed.

Mark heard it, too. A wild crashing in the overgrown tangle of rhododendrons and blackberry bushes at the back of the garden. It was a weird, frenzied sound, but Jade's reaction was out of all proportion. She had frozen, body tense and trembling, eyes fixed on the underbrush. She looked terrified.

"Hey." Mark spoke gently, then touched her shoulder. "Hey. It's all right. It's probably one of the goats that got loose; goats can jump over any kind of fence." She was shaking her head. "Or a deer. When they're relaxed they sound just like people walking."

"It's not a deer," she hissed.

"They come down and eat people's gardens at night. You probably don't have deer roaming around where you come from—"

"I can't *smell* anything," she said in a kind of whispered wail. "It's that stupid pen. Everything smells like *goat.*"

She couldn't smell . . . ? Mark did the only thing he could think of in response to a statement like that. He put his arms around the girl.

"Everything's okay," he said softly. He couldn't help but

notice that she was cool and warm at the same time, supple, wonderfully alive underneath the nightshirt. "Why don't I take you inside now? You'll be safe there."

"Leggo," Jade said ungratefully, squirming. "I may have to fight." She wriggled out of his arms and faced the bushes again. "Stay behind me."

Okay, so she *is* crazy. I don't care. I think I love her.

He stood beside her. "Look, I'll fight, too. What do you think it is? Bear, coyote . . . ?"

"My brother."

"Your . . ." Dismay pooled in Mark. She'd just stepped over the line of acceptable craziness. "Oh."

Another thrashing sound from the bushes. It was definitely something big, not a goat. Mark was just wondering vaguely if a Roosevelt elk could have wandered down the hundred or so miles from Waldo Lake, when a scream ripped through the air.

A human scream—or, worse, *almost* human. As it died, there was a wail that was definitely inhuman—it started out faint, and then suddenly sounded shrill and close. Mark was stunned. When the drawn-out wail finally stopped, there was a sobbing, moaning sound, then silence.

Mark got his breath and swore. "What in the—what *was* that?"

"Shh. Keep still." Jade was in a half-crouch, eyes on the bushes.

"Jade—Jade, listen. We've got to get inside." Desperate, he looped an arm around her waist, trying to pick her up. She was light, but she flowed like water out of his arms. Like a cat that doesn't want to be petted. "Jade, whatever that thing is, we need a *gun*."

"I don't." She seemed to be speaking through her teeth—anyway there was something odd about her diction. She had her back to him and he couldn't see her face, but her hands were clawed.

"Jade," Mark said urgently. He was scared enough to run, but he couldn't leave her. He *couldn't.* No good guy would do that.

Too late. The blackberry bushes to the south quivered. Parted. Something was coming through.

Mark's heart seemed to freeze solid, but then he found himself moving. Pushing Jade roughly aside. Standing in front of her to face whatever the thing in the dark was.

Mary-Lynnette kicked her way through the blackberry canes. Her arms and legs were scratched, and she could feel ripe, bright-black berries squishing against her. She'd probably picked a bad place to get through the hedge, but she hadn't been thinking about that. She'd been thinking about Mark, about finding him as fast as possible and getting away from here.

Just please let him be here, she thought. Let him be here and be okay and I'll never ask for anything else.

She struggled through the last of the canes into the backyard—and then things happened very fast. The first thing she saw was Mark, and she felt a rush of relief. Then a flash of surprise. Mark was standing in front of a girl, his arms lifted like a basketball guard. As if to protect her from Mary-Lynnette.

And then, so quickly that Mary-Lynnette could barely follow the motion, the girl was rushing at her. And Mary-Lynnette was throwing her arms up and Mark was shouting, "No, that's my sister!"

The girl stopped a foot away from Mary-Lynnette. It was the little silvery-haired one, of course. This close Mary-Lynnette could see that she had green eyes and skin so translucent it almost looked like quartz crystal.

"Jade, it's my sister," Mark said again, as if anxious to get this established. "Her name's Mary-Lynnette. She won't hurt you. Mare, tell her you won't hurt her."

Hurt her? Mary-Lynnette didn't know what he was talking about, and didn't want to. This girl was as weirdly beautiful as the others, and something about her eyes—they weren't ordinary green, but almost silvery—made Mary-Lynnette's skin rise in goose pimples.

"Hello," Jade said.

"Hello. Okay, Mark, c'mon. We've got to go. Like, right now."

She expected him to agree immediately. He was the one who hadn't wanted to come, and now here he was with his most dreaded phobia, a girl. But instead he said, "Did you hear that yelling? Could you tell where it came from?"

"What yelling? I was inside. Come on." Mary-Lynnette took Mark's arm, but since he was as strong as she was, it didn't do any good. "Maybe I heard something. I wasn't paying attention." She'd been looking desperately around the Victorian living room, babbling out lies about how her family knew where she'd gone tonight and expected her back soon. How her father and stepmother were such good friends of Mrs. Burdock's and how they were just waiting at home to hear about Mrs. B.'s nieces. She still wasn't sure if that was why they'd let her go. But for some reason, Rowan had finally stood up, given Mary-Lynnette a grave, sweet smile, and opened the front door.

"You know, I bet it was a wolverine," Mark was saying to Jade excitedly. "A wolverine that came down from Willamette Forest."

Jade was frowning. "A wolverine?" She considered. "Yeah, I guess that could have been it. I've never heard one before." She looked at Mary-Lynnette. "Is that what you think it was?"

"Oh, sure," Mary-Lynnette said at random. "Definitely a wolverine." I should ask where her aunt is, she thought suddenly. It's the perfect opportunity to catch her in a lie. I'll ask and then she'll say something—anything, but not that her aunt's gone up north for a little vacation on the coast. And then I'll *know.*

She didn't do it. She simply didn't have the courage. She

didn't want to catch anyone in a lie anymore; she just wanted to get out.

"Mark, please . . ."

He looked at her and for the first time seemed to see how upset she was. "Uh—okay," he said. And to Jade: "Look, why don't you go back inside now? You'll be safe there. And maybe—maybe I could come over again sometime?"

Mary-Lynnette was still tugging at him, and now, to her relief, he began to move. Mary-Lynnette headed for the blackberry bushes that she'd trampled coming in.

"Why don't you go through there? It's like a path," Jade said, pointing. Mark immediately swerved, taking Mary-Lynnette with him, and she saw a comfortable gap between two rhododendron bushes at the back of the garden. She would never have seen it unless she knew what to look for.

As they reached the hedge, Mark turned to glance behind him. Mary-Lynnette turned, too.

From here, Jade was just a dark silhouette against the porch light—but her hair, lit from behind, looked like a silver halo. It shimmered around her. Mary-Lynnette heard Mark draw in his breath.

"You both come back sometime," Jade said cordially. "Help us milk the goats like Aunt Opal said. She gave us *very* strict orders before she went on vacation."

Mary-Lynnette was dumbfounded.

She turned back and reeled through the gap, her head

spinning. When they got to the road, she said, "Mark, what happened when you got into the garden?"

Mark was looking preoccupied. "What do you mean what happened? Nothing happened."

"Did you look at the place that was dug up?"

"No," Mark said shortly. "Jade was in the garden when I got there. I didn't get a chance to look at anything."

"Mark . . . was she there the whole time? Jade? Did she ever go in the house? Or did either of the other girls ever come out?"

Mark grunted. "I don't even know what the other girls look like. The only one I saw was Jade, and she was there the whole time." He looked at her darkly. "You're not still on this *Rear Window* thing, are you?"

Mary-Lynnette didn't answer. She was trying to gather her scattered thoughts.

I don't believe it. But she *said* it. Orders about the goats. Before her aunt went on vacation.

But Rowan didn't know about the goats before I told her. I'd *swear* she didn't know. And I was so sure she was winging it with the vacation business. . . .

Okay, maybe I was wrong. But that doesn't mean Rowan was telling the truth. Maybe they *did* figure the story out before tonight, and Rowan's just a lousy actress. Or maybe . . .

"Mark, this is going to sound crazy . . . but Jade didn't have, like, a cellular phone or anything, did she?"

Mark stopped dead and gave Mary-Lynnette a long, slow look that said more clearly than words what he thought of this. "Mary-Lynnette, what's *wrong* with you?"

"Rowan and Kestrel told me that Mrs. B. is on vacation. That she suddenly *decided* to take a vacation just when they arrived in town."

"So? Jade said the same thing."

"Mark, Mrs. B. has lived there for ten years, and she's *never* taken a vacation. Never. How could she take one starting the same day her nieces come to live with her?"

"Maybe because they can house-sit for her," Mark said with devastating logic.

It was exactly what Rowan had said. Mary-Lynnette had a sudden feeling of paranoia, like someone who realizes that everyone around her is a pod person, all in on the conspiracy. She had been about to tell him about the goats, but now she didn't want to.

Oh, get a *grip* on yourself, girl. Even Mark is being logical. The least you can do is think about this rationally before you run to Sheriff Akers.

The fact is, Mary-Lynnette told herself, brutally honest, that you panicked. You got a *feeling* about those girls for some reason, and then you forgot logic completely. You didn't get any kind of hard evidence. You ran away.

She could hardly go to the sheriff and say that she was suspicious because Rowan had creepy feet.

There's no evidence at all. Nothing except . . .

She groaned inwardly.

"It all comes down to what's in the garden," she said out loud.

Mark, who had been walking beside her in frowning silence, now stopped. "What?"

"It all comes back to that again," Mary-Lynnette said, her eyes shut. "I should have just looked at that dug-up place when I had the chance, even if Jade saw me. It's the only real evidence there is . . . so I've got to see what's there."

Mark was shaking his head. "Now, look—"

"I have to go back. Not tonight. I'm dead tired. But tomorrow. Mark, I *have* to check it out before I go to Sheriff Akers."

Mark exploded.

"Before you *what*?" he shouted, loud enough to raise echoes. "What are you *talking* about, going to the sheriff?"

Mary-Lynnette stared. She hadn't realized how different Mark's point of view was from hers. Why, she thought, why he's . . .

"You wanted to check out where Mrs. B. was—so we checked where Mrs. B. was," Mark said. "They *told* us where. And you *saw* Jade. I know she's a little different—it's like you said about Mrs. B.; she's eccentric. But did she look like the kind of person who could hurt somebody? Well, *did* she?"

Why, he's in love with her, Mary-Lynnette thought. Or at least seriously in like. Mark likes a girl.

Now she was *really* confused.

This could be so good for him—if only the girl weren't crazy. Well, maybe even if the girl was crazy—if it wasn't a homicidal craziness. Either way, Mary-Lynnette couldn't call the police on Mark's new girlfriend unless she had some evidence.

I wonder if she likes him, too? she thought. They certainly seemed to be protecting each other when I walked in.

"No, you're right," she said aloud, glad that she'd had practice lying tonight. "She doesn't look like the kind of person who could hurt somebody. I'll just let it drop."

With you. And tomorrow night when you think I'm star-watching, I'll sneak over there. This time bringing my own shovel. And maybe a big stick to fend off wolverines.

"Do you really think you heard a wolverine over there?" she asked, to change the subject.

"Um . . . maybe." Mark was slowly losing his scowl. "It was *something* weird. Something I've never heard before. So you're going to forget all this crazy stuff about Mrs. B., right?"

"Yeah, I am." I'll be safe, Mary-Lynnette was thinking. This time I won't panic, and I'll make sure they don't see me. Besides, if they were going to kill me, they would have done it tonight, wouldn't they?

"Maybe it was Sasquatch we heard yelling," Mark said.

CHAPTER 6

"Why didn't we just kill her?" Kestrel asked.

Rowan and Jade looked at each other. There were few things they agreed on, but one of them was definitely Kestrel.

"First of all, we agreed not to do that here. We don't use our powers—"

"And we don't feed on humans. Or kill them," Kestrel finished the chant. "But you already used your powers tonight; you called Jade."

"I had to let her know what story I'd just told about Aunt Opal. Actually, I should have planned for this earlier. I should have realized that people are going to come and ask where Aunt Opal is."

"*She's* the only one who's asking. If we killed her—"

"We can't just go killing people in our new home," Rowan said tightly. "Besides, she said she had family waiting for her. Are we going to kill all of them?"

Kestrel shrugged.

"We are *not* going to start a blood feud," Rowan said even more tightly.

"But what about influencing her?" Jade said. She was sitting with Tiggy in her arms, kissing the velvety black top of the kitten's head. "Making her forget she's suspicious—or making her think she *saw* Aunt Opal?"

"That would be fine—if it were just her," Rowan said patiently. "But it's not. Are we going to influence *everyone* who comes to the house? What about people who call on the phone? What about teachers? You two are supposed to start school in a couple of weeks."

"Maybe we'll just have to miss that," Kestrel said without regret.

Rowan was shaking her head. "We need a permanent solution. We need to find some reasonable explanation for why Aunt Opal is gone."

"We need to move Aunt Opal," Kestrel said flatly. "We need to get rid of her."

"No, no. We might have to produce the *body*," Rowan said.

"Looking like *that*?"

They began to argue about it. Jade rested her chin on Tiggy's head and stared out the multipaned kitchen window. She was thinking about Mark Carter, who had such a gallant heart. It gave her a pleasantly forbidden thrill just to picture him. Back home there weren't any humans wandering around free. She could never have been tempted to break Night World law and fall in love with one. But here . . . yes, Jade could almost imagine falling in love with Mark Carter. Just as if she were a human girl.

She shivered deliriously. But just as she was trying to picture what human girls did when they were in love, Tiggy gave a sudden heave. He twisted out of her arms and hit the kitchen floor running. The fur on his back was up.

Jade looked at the window again. She couldn't see anything. But . . . she *felt* . . .

She turned to her sisters. "Something was out there in the garden tonight," she said. "And I couldn't smell it."

Rowan and Kestrel were still arguing. They didn't hear her.

Mary-Lynnette opened her eyes and sneezed. She'd overslept. Sun was shining around the edges of her dark blue curtains.

Get up and get to work, she told herself. But instead she lay rubbing sleep out of her eyes and trying to wake up. She was a night person, not a morning person.

The room was large and painted twilight blue. Mary-Lynnette had stuck the glow-in-the-dark stars and planets to the ceiling herself. Taped onto the dresser mirror was a bumper sticker saying I BRAKE FOR ASTEROIDS. On the walls were a giant relief map of the moon, a poster from the *Skygazer's Almanac,* and photographic prints of the Pleiades, the Horsehead Nebula, and the total eclipse of 1995.

It was Mary-Lynnette's retreat, the place to go when people didn't understand. She always felt safe in the night.

She yawned and staggered to the bathroom, grabbing a pair of jeans and a T-shirt on the way. She was brushing her hair as she walked down the stairs when she heard voices from the living room.

Claudine's voice . . . and a male voice. Not Mark; weekdays he usually went to his friend Ben's house. A stranger.

Mary-Lynnette peeked through the kitchen. There was a guy sitting on the living room couch. She could see only the back of his head, which was ash blond. Mary-Lynnette shrugged and started to open the refrigerator, when she heard her own name.

"Mary-Lynnette is very good friends with her," Claudine was saying in her quick, lightly accented voice. "I remember a few years ago she helped her fix up a goat shed."

They're talking about Mrs. B.!

"Why does she keep goats? I think she told Mary-Lynnette it would help since she couldn't get out that much anymore."

"How strange," the guy said. He had a lazy, careless-sounding voice. "I wonder what she meant by that."

Mary-Lynnette, who was now peering intently through the kitchen while keeping absolutely still, saw Claudine give one of her slight, charming shrugs.

"I suppose she meant the milk—every day she has fresh milk now. She doesn't have to go to the store. But I don't know. You'll have to ask her yourself." She laughed.

Not going to be easy, Mary-Lynnette thought. Now, why would some strange guy be here asking questions about Mrs. B.?

Of course. He had to be police or something. FBI. But his voice made her wonder. He sounded too young to be either, unless he was planning to infiltrate Dewitt High as a narc. Mary-Lynnette edged farther into the kitchen, getting a better view. There—she could see him in the mirror.

Disappointment coursed through her.

Definitely not old enough to be FBI. And much as Mary-Lynnette wanted him to be a keen-eyed, quick-witted, hard-driving detective, he wasn't. He was only the handsomest boy she'd ever seen in her life.

He was lanky and elegant, with long legs stretched out in front of him, ankles crossed under the coffee table. He looked like a big amiable cat. He had clean-cut features, slightly tilted wicked eyes, and a disarming lazy grin.

Not just lazy, Mary-Lynnette decided. Fatuous. Bland. Maybe even stupid. She wasn't impressed by good looks unless they were the thin, brown, and interesting kind, like—well, like Jeremy Lovett for instance. Gorgeous guys—guys who looked like big ash-blond cats—didn't have any reason to develop their minds. They were self-absorbed and vain. With IQs barely high enough to keep a seat warm.

And this guy looked as if he couldn't get awake or serious to save his life.

I don't care what he's here for. I think I'll go upstairs.

It was then that the guy on the couch lifted one hand, wiggling the fingers in the air. He half-turned. Not far enough actually to look at Mary-Lynnette, but far enough to make it clear he was talking to somebody behind him. She could now see his profile in the mirror. "Hi, there."

"Mary-Lynnette, is that you?" Claudine called.

"Yes." Mary-Lynnette opened the refrigerator door and made banging noises. "Just getting some juice. Then I'm going out."

Her heart was beating hard—with embarrassment and annoyance. Okay, so he must have seen her in the mirror. He probably thought she was staring at him because of the way he looked. He probably had people staring at him everywhere he went. So what, big deal, go away.

"Don't go yet," Claudine called. "Come out here and talk for a few minutes."

No. Mary-Lynnette knew it was a childish and stupid reaction, but she couldn't help it. She banged a bottle of apricot juice against a bottle of Calistoga sparkling water.

"Come meet Mrs. Burdock's nephew," Claudine called.

Mary-Lynnette went still.

She stood in the cold air of the refrigerator, looking sightlessly at the temperature dial in the back. Then she put the bottle of apricot juice down. She twisted a Coke out of a six-pack without seeing it.

What nephew? I don't remember hearing about any nephew.

But then, she'd never heard much about Mrs. B.'s nieces either, not until they were coming out. Mrs. B. just didn't talk about her family much.

So he's her nephew . . . *that's* why he's asking about her. But does he *know*? Is he in on it with those girls? Or is he after them? Or . . .

Thoroughly confused, she walked into the living room.

"Mary-Lynnette, this is Ash. He's here to visit with his aunt and his sisters," Claudine said. "Ash, this is Mary-Lynnette. The one who's such good friends with your aunt."

Ash got up, all in one lovely, lazy motion. Just like a cat, including the stretch in the middle. "Hi."

He offered a hand. Mary-Lynnette touched it with fingers damp and cold from the Coke can, glanced up at his face, and said "Hi."

Except that it didn't happen that way.

It happened like this: Mary-Lynnette had her eyes on the carpet as she came in, which gave her a good view of his Nike tennis shoes and the ripped knees of his jeans. When he stood up she looked at his T-shirt, which had an obscure design—a black flower on a white background. Probably the emblem of some rock group. And then when his hand entered her field of vision, she reached for it automatically, muttering a greeting and looking up at his face just as she touched it. And—

This was the part that was hard to describe.

Contact.

Something happened.

Hey, don't I *know* you?

She didn't. That was the thing. She didn't know him—but she felt that she should. She also felt as if somebody had reached inside her and touched her spine with a live electric wire. It was extremely not-enjoyable. The room turned vaguely pink. Her throat swelled and she could feel her heart beating there. Also not-enjoyable. But somehow when you put it all together, it made a kind of trembly dizziness like . . .

Like what she felt when she looked at the Lagoon Nebula. Or imagined galaxies gathered into clusters and superclusters, bigger and bigger, until size lost any meaning and she felt herself falling.

She was falling now. She couldn't see anything except his eyes. And those eyes were strange, prismlike, changing color like a star seen through heavy atmosphere. Now blue, now gold, now violet.

Oh, take this away. Please, I don't *want* it.

"It's so good to see a new face around here, isn't it? We're very boring out here by ourselves," Claudine said, in completely normal and slightly flustered tones. Mary-Lynnette was snapped out of her trance, and she reacted as if Ash had just offered her a mongoose instead of his hand. She jumped backward, looking anywhere but at him. She had the feeling of being saved from falling down a mine shaft.

"O-kay," Claudine said in her cute accent. "Hmm." She was twisting a strand of curly dark hair, something she only did when she was extremely nervous. "Maybe you guys know each other already?"

There was a silence.

I should say something, Mary-Lynnette thought dazedly, staring at the fieldstone fireplace. I'm acting crazy and humiliating Claudine.

But what just happened here?

Doesn't matter. Worry later. She swallowed, plastered a smile on her face, and said, "So, how long are you here for?"

Her mistake was that then she looked at him. And it all happened again. Not quite as vividly as before, maybe because she wasn't touching him. But the electric shock feeling was the same.

And *he* looked like a cat who's had a shock. Bristling. Unhappy. Astonished. Well, at least he was awake, Mary-Lynnette thought. He and Mary-Lynnette stared at each other while the room spun and turned pink.

"Who *are* you?" Mary-Lynnette said, abandoning any vestige of politeness.

"Who are *you*?" he said, in just about exactly the same tone.

They both glared.

Claudine was making little clicking noises with her tongue and clearing away the tomato juice. Mary-Lynnette felt distantly sorry for her, but couldn't spare her any attention. Mary-Lynnette's whole consciousness was focused on the guy in front of her; on fighting him, on blocking him out. On getting rid of this bizarre feeling that she was one of two puzzle pieces that had just been snapped together.

"Now, look," she said tensely, at the precise moment that he began brusquely, "Look—"

They both stopped and glared again. Then Mary-Lynnette managed to tear her eyes away. Something was tugging at her mind. . . .

"Ash," she said, getting hold of it. "*Ash.* Mrs. Burdock *did* say something about you . . . about a little boy named Ash. I didn't know she was talking about her nephew."

"Great-nephew," Ash said, his voice not quite steady. "What did she say?"

"She said that you were a bad little boy, and that you were probably going to grow up even worse."

"Well, she had *that* right," Ash said, and his expression softened a bit—as if he were on more familiar ground.

Mary-Lynnette's heart was slowing. She found that if she concentrated, she could make the strange feelings recede. It helped if she looked away from Ash.

Deep breath, she told herself. And another. Okay, now let's get things straight. Let go of what just happened; forget all that; think about it later. What's important *now*?

What was important *now* was that: 1) This guy was the brother of those girls; 2) He might be in on whatever had happened to Mrs. B.; and 3) If he *wasn't* in on it, he might be able to help with some information. Such as whether his aunt had left a will, and if so, who got the family jewels.

She glanced at Ash from the side of her eye. He definitely looked calmer. Hackles going down. Chest lifting more slowly. They were both switching gear.

"So Rowan and Kestrel and Jade are your sisters," she said, with all the polite nonchalance she could muster. "They seem—nice."

"I didn't know you knew them," Claudine said, and Mary-Lynnette realized her stepmother was hovering in the doorway, petite shoulder against the doorjamb, arms crossed, dish towel in hand. "I told him you hadn't met them."

"Mark and I went over there yesterday," Mary-Lynnette said. And when she said it, something flashed in Ash's face—something there and gone before she could really analyze it. But it made her feel as if she were standing on the edge of a cliff in a cold wind.

Why? What could be wrong with mentioning she'd met the girls?

"You and Mark . . . and Mark would be—your brother?"

"That's right," Claudine said from the doorway.

"Any other brothers or sisters?"

Mary-Lynnette blinked. "What, you're taking a census?"

Ash did a bad imitation of his former lazy smile. "I just like to keep track of my sisters' friends."

Why? "To see if you approve or something?"

"Actually, yes." He did the smile again, with more success. "We're an old-fashioned family. Very old-fashioned."

Mary-Lynnette's jaw dropped. Then, all at once, she felt happy. Now she didn't need to think about murders or pink rooms or what this guy knew. All she needed to think about was what she was going to do to him.

"So you're an old-fashioned family," she said, moving a step forward.

Ash nodded.

"And you're in charge," Mary-Lynnette said.

"Well, out here. Back home, my father is."

"And you're just going to tell your sisters which friends they can have. Maybe you get to decide your aunt's friends, too?"

"Actually, I was just discussing that. . . ." He waved a hand toward Claudine.

Yes, you were, Mary-Lynnette realized. She took another step toward Ash, who was still smiling.

"Oh, no," Claudine said. She flapped her dish towel once. "Don't smile."

"I like a girl with spirit," Ash offered, as if he'd worked hard on finding the most obnoxious thing possible to say.

Then, with a sort of determined bravado, he winked, reached out, and chucked Mary-Lynnette under the chin.

Fzzz! Sparks. Mary-Lynnette sprang back. So did Ash, looking at his own hand as if it had betrayed him.

Mary-Lynnette had an inexplicable impulse to knock Ash flat and fall down on top of him. She'd never felt *that* for any boy before.

She ignored the impulse and kicked him in the shin.

He yelped and hopped backward. Once again the sleepy smugness was gone from his face. He looked alarmed.

"I think you'd better go away now," Mary-Lynnette said pleasantly. She was amazed at herself. She'd never been the violent type. Maybe there were things hidden deep inside her that she'd never suspected.

Claudine was gasping and shaking her head. Ash was still hopping, but not going anywhere. Mary-Lynnette advanced on him again. Even though he was half a head taller, he backed up. He stared at her in something like wonder.

"Hey. Hey, look, you know, you really don't know what you're doing," he said. "If you knew . . ." And Mary-Lynnette saw it again—something in his face that made him suddenly look not fatuous or amiable at all. Like the glitter of a knife blade in the light. Something that said *danger*. . . .

"Oh, go bother someone *else*," Mary-Lynnette said. She drew back her foot for another kick.

He opened his mouth, then shut it. Still holding his shin,

he looked at Claudine and managed a hurt and miserable flirtatious smile.

"Thanks so much for all your—"

"Go!"

He lost the smile. "That's what I'm doing!" He limped to the front door. She followed him.

"What do they call you, anyway?" he asked from the front yard, as if he'd finally found the comeback he'd been looking for. "Mary? Marylin? M'lin? M.L.?"

"They call me Mary-Lynnette," Mary-Lynnette said flatly, and added under her breath, "That do speak of me." She'd read *The Taming of the Shrew* in honors English last year.

"Oh, yeah? How about M'lin the cursed?" He was still backing away.

Mary-Lynnette was startled. So maybe his class had read it, too. But he didn't look smart enough to quote Shakespeare.

"Have fun with your sisters," she said, and shut the door. Then she leaned against it, trying to get her breath. Her fingers and face were prickly-numb, as if she were going to faint.

If those girls had only murdered *him*, I'd understand, she thought. But they're *all* so strange—there's something seriously weird about that whole family.

Weird in a way that scared her. If she'd believed in premonitions, she'd have been even more scared. She had a bad feeling—a feeling that *things* were going to happen. . . .

Claudine was staring at her from the living room. "Very

fabulous," she said. "You've just kicked a guest. Now, what was that all *about*?"

"He wouldn't leave."

"You know what I mean. Do you two know each other?"

Mary-Lynnette just shrugged vaguely. The dizziness was passing, but her mind was swimming with questions.

Claudine looked at her intently, then shook her head. "I remember my little brother—when he was four years old he used to push a girl flat on her face in the sandbox. He did it to show he liked her."

Mary-Lynnette ignored this. "Claude—what was Ash *here* for? What did you talk about?"

"About nothing," Claudine said, exasperated. "Just ordinary conversation. Since you hate him so much, what difference does it make?" Then, as Mary-Lynnette kept looking at her, she sighed. "He was very interested in weird facts about life in the country. All the local stories."

Mary-Lynnette snorted. "Did you tell him about Sasquatch?"

"I told him about Vic and Todd."

Mary-Lynnette froze. "You're joking. Why?"

"Because that's the kind of thing he asked about! People lost in time—"

"Losing time."

"Whatever. We were just having a nice conversation. He was a nice boy. *Finis.*"

Mary-Lynnette's heart was beating fast.

She was right. She was sure of it now. Todd and Vic *were* connected to whatever had happened with the sisters and Mrs. B. But what was the connection?

I'm going to go and find out, she thought.

CHAPTER 7

Finding Todd and Vic turned out not to be easy.

It was late afternoon by the time Mary-Lynnette walked into the Briar Creek general store, which sold everything from nails to nylons to canned peas.

"Hi, Bunny. I don't suppose you've seen Todd or Vic around?"

Bunny Marten looked up from behind the counter. She was pretty, with soft blond hair, a round, dimpled face, and a timid expression. She was in Mary-Lynnette's class at school. "Did you check over at the Gold Creek Bar?"

Mary-Lynnette nodded. "And at their houses, and at the other store, and at the sheriff's office." The sheriff's office was also city hall and the public library.

"Well, if they're not playing pool, they're usually plinking." Plinking was shooting at cans for practice.

"Yeah, but where?" Mary-Lynnette said.

Bunny shook her head, earrings glinting. "Your guess is as good as mine." She hesitated, staring down at her cuticles, which she was pushing back with a little blunt-pointed wooden stick. "But, you know, I've heard they go down to Mad Dog Creek sometimes." Her wide blue eyes lifted to Mary-Lynnette's meaningfully.

Mad Dog Creek . . . Oh, great. Mary-Lynnette grimaced.

"I know." Bunny raised her shoulders in a shiver. "*I* wouldn't go down there. I'd be thinking about that body the whole time."

"Yeah, me, too. Well, thanks, Bun. See you."

Bunny examined her cuticles critically. "Good hunting," she said absently.

Mary-Lynnette went out of the store, squinting in the hot, hazy August sunlight. Main Street wasn't big. It had a handful of brick and stone buildings from the days when Briar Creek had been a gold rush supply town, and a few modern frame buildings with peeling paint. Todd and Vic weren't in any of them.

Well, what now? Mary-Lynnette sighed. There was no road to Mad Dog Creek, only a trail that was constantly blocked by new growth and deadfall. And everyone knew more than plinking went on there.

If they're out there, they're probably hunting, she thought. Not to mention drinking, maybe using drugs. Guns and beer. And then there's that body.

The body had been found last year around this time. A man; a hiker, from his backpack. Nobody knew who he was or how he'd died—the corpse was too desiccated and chewed by animals to tell. But people talked about ghosts floating around the creek last winter.

Mary-Lynnette sighed again and got into her station wagon.

The car was ancient, it was rusty, it made alarming sounds when forced to accelerate, but it was *hers*, and Mary-Lynnette did her best to keep it alive. She loved it because there was plenty of room in back to store her telescope.

At Briar Creek's only gas station she fished a scrolled fruit knife from under the seat and went to work, prying at the rusty gas cap cover.

A little higher up . . . almost, almost . . . now *twist* . . .

The cover flew open.

"Ever think of going into the safecracking business?" a voice behind her said. "You've got the touch."

Mary-Lynnette turned. "Hi, Jeremy."

He smiled—a smile that showed mostly in his eyes, which were clear brown with outrageously dark lashes.

If I were going to fall for a guy—and I'm not—it would be for somebody like him. *Not* for a big blond cat who thinks he can pick his sisters' friends.

It was a moot point, anyway—Jeremy didn't go out with girls. He was a loner.

"Want me to look under the hood?" He wiped his hands on a rag.

"No, thanks. I just checked everything last week." Mary-Lynnette started to pump gas.

He picked up a squeegee and a spray bottle and began to wash the windshield. His movements were deft and gentle and his face was utterly solemn.

Mary-Lynnette had to swallow a giggle herself, but she appreciated him not laughing at the pitted glass and corroded windshield wipers. She'd always had an odd feeling of kinship with Jeremy. He was the only person in Briar Creek who seemed even slightly interested in astronomy—he'd helped her build a model of the solar system in eighth grade, and of course he'd watched last year's lunar eclipse with her.

His parents had died in Medford when he was just a baby, and his uncle brought him to Briar Creek in a Fleetwood trailer. The uncle was strange—always wandering off to dowse for gold in the Klamath wilderness. One day he didn't come back.

After that, Jeremy lived alone in the trailer in the woods. He did odd jobs and worked at the gas station to make money. And if his clothes weren't as nice as some of the other kids', he didn't care—or he didn't let it show.

The handle of the gas hose clicked in Mary-Lynnette's hand. She realized she had been daydreaming.

"Anything else?" Jeremy said. The windshield was clean.

"No . . . well, actually, yes. You haven't, um, seen Todd Akers or Vic Kimble today, have you?"

Jeremy paused in the middle of taking her twenty-dollar bill. "Why?"

"I just wanted to talk to them," Mary-Lynnette said. She could feel heat in her cheeks. Oh, God, he thinks I want to see Todd and Vic socially—and he thinks I'm crazy for asking *him.*

She hurried to explain. "It's just that Bunny said they might be down by Mad Dog Creek, so I thought you might have seen them, maybe sometime this morning, since you live down around there. . . ."

Jeremy shook his head. "I left at noon, but I didn't hear any gunshots from the creek this morning. Actually, I don't think they've been there all summer—I keep telling them to stay away."

He said it quietly, without emphasis, but Mary-Lynnette had the sudden feeling that maybe even Todd and Vic might listen to him. She'd never known Jeremy to get in a fight. But sometimes a look came into his level brown eyes that was . . . almost frightening. As if there was something underneath that quiet-guy exterior—something primitive and pure and deadly that could do a lot of damage if roused.

"Mary-Lynnette—I know you probably think this is none of my business, but . . . well, I think you should stay away from those guys. If you really want to go find them, let me go with you."

Oh. Mary-Lynnette felt a warm flush of gratitude. She wouldn't take him up on the offer . . . but it was nice of him to make it.

"Thanks," she said. "I'll be fine, but . . . thanks."

She watched as he went to get her change inside the station. What must it feel like to be on your own since you were twelve years old? Maybe he needed help. Maybe she should ask her dad to offer him some odd jobs around the house. He did them for everyone else. She just had to be careful—she knew Jeremy hated anything that smacked of charity.

He brought back the change. "Here you go. And, Mary-Lynnette . . ."

She looked up.

"If you do find Todd and Vic, be careful."

"I know."

"I mean it."

"I know," Mary-Lynnette said. She had reached for the change, but he hadn't let go of it. Instead, he did something odd: He opened her curled fingers with one hand while giving her the bills and coins with the other. Then he curled her fingers back over it. In effect, he was holding her hand.

The moment of physical contact surprised her—and touched her. She found herself looking at his thin brown fingers, at their strong but delicate grip on her hand, at the gold seal ring with the black design that he wore.

She was even more surprised when she glanced up at his

face again. There was open concern in his eyes—and something like respect. For an instant she had a wild and completely inexplicable impulse to tell him everything. But she could just imagine what he would think. Jeremy was very practical.

"Thanks, Jeremy," she said, conjuring up a weak smile. "Take care."

"*You* take care. There are people who'd miss you if anything happened." He smiled, but she could feel his worried gaze on her even as she drove away.

All right, *now* what?

Well, she'd wasted most of the day looking for Todd and Vic. And now, with the image of Jeremy's level brown eyes in her mind, she wondered if it had been a stupid idea from the beginning.

Brown eyes . . . and what color eyes did the big blond cat have? Strange, it was hard to remember. She thought that they had looked brown at one point—when he was talking about his old-fashioned family. But when he'd said he liked a girl with spirit, she remembered them being a sort of insipid blue. And when that odd knife-glint had flashed in them, hadn't they been icy gray?

Oh, who *cares*? Maybe they were orange. Let's just go home now. Get ready for tonight.

How come Nancy Drew always found the people she wanted to interrogate?

• • •

Why? Why? Why me?

Ash was staring at a yellow cedar weeping into a creek. A squirrel too stupid to get out of the sun was staring back at him. On a rock beside him a lizard lifted first one foot, then another.

It wasn't fair. It wasn't right.

He didn't even believe it.

He'd always been lucky. Or at least he'd always managed to escape a hairsbreadth away from disaster. But this time the disaster had hit and it was a total annihilation.

Everything he was, everything he believed about himself . . . could he lose that in five minutes? For a girl who was probably deranged and certainly more dangerous than all three of his sisters put together?

No, he concluded grimly. Absolutely not. Not in five minutes. It only took five seconds.

He knew so many girls—nice girls. Witches with mysterious smiles, vampires with delicious curves, shapeshifters with cute furry tails. Even human girls with fancy sports cars who never seemed to mind when he nibbled their necks. Why couldn't it have been one of them?

Well, it wasn't. And there was no point in wondering about the injustice of it. The question was, what was he going to *do* about it? Just sit back and let fate ride over him like an eighteen-wheeler?

I'm sorry for your family, Quinn had said to him. And maybe that was the problem. Ash was a victim of his Redfern genes. Redferns never could stay out of trouble; they seemed to tangle with humans at every turn.

So was he going to wait for Quinn to come back and then offer that as an excuse? I'm sorry; I can't handle things here after all; I can't even finish the investigation.

If he did that, Quinn would call in the Elders and they would investigate for themselves.

Ash felt his expression harden. He narrowed his eyes at the squirrel, which suddenly darted for the tree in a flash of red fur. Beside him, the lizard stopped moving.

No, he wasn't just going to wait for fate to finish him off. He'd do what he could to salvage the situation—and the family honor.

He'd do it tonight.

"We'll do it tonight," Rowan said. "After it's fully dark; before the moon rises. We'll move her to the forest."

Kestrel smiled magnanimously. She'd won the argument.

"We'll have to be careful," Jade said. "That thing I heard outside last night—it wasn't an animal. I think it was one of *us*."

"There aren't any other Night People around here," Rowan said gently. "That was the whole point of coming here in the first place."

"Maybe it was a vampire hunter," Kestrel said. "Maybe the one that killed Aunt Opal."

"*If* a vampire hunter killed Aunt Opal," Rowan said. "We don't know that. Tomorrow we should look around town, see if we can at least get an idea who *might* have done it."

"And when we find them, we'll take care of them," Jade said fiercely.

"And if the thing you heard in the garden turns up, we'll take care of it, too," Kestrel said. She smiled, a hungry smile.

Twilight, and Mary-Lynnette was watching the clock. The rest of her family was comfortably settled in for the night; her father reading a book about World War II, Claudine working conscientiously on a needlepoint project, Mark trying to tune up his old guitar that had been sitting in the basement for years. He was undoubtedly trying to think of words to rhyme with *Jade.*

Mary-Lynnette's father looked up from his book. "Going starwatching?"

"Yup. It should be a good night—no moon till after midnight. It's the last chance to see some Perseids." She wasn't exactly lying. It *would* be a good night, and she could keep an eye out for stragglers from the Perseid meteor storm as she walked to Burdock Farm.

"Okay; just be careful," her father said.

Mary-Lynnette was surprised. He hadn't said anything like

that for years. She glanced at Claudine, who jabbed with her needle, lips pursed.

"Maybe Mark should go with you," Claudine said, without looking up.

Oh, God, she thinks I'm unstable, Mary-Lynnette thought. I don't really blame her.

"No, no. I'll be fine. I'll be careful." She said it too quickly.

Mark's eyes narrowed. "Don't you need any help with your stuff?"

"No, I'll take the car. I'll be fine. *Really.*" Mary-Lynnette fled to the garage before her family could come up with anything else.

She didn't pack her telescope. Instead, she put a shovel in the backseat. She looped the strap of her camera around her neck and stuck a pen flashlight in her pocket.

She parked at the foot of her hill. Before she got the shovel out, she paused a moment to look dutifully northeast, toward the constellation Perseus.

No meteors right this second. All right. Keys in hand, she turned to open the back of the station wagon—and jumped violently.

"Oh, God!"

She'd nearly walked into Ash.

"Hi."

Mary-Lynnette's pulse was racing and her knees felt weak. From fear, she told herself. And that's *all.*

"You nearly gave me a heart attack!" she said. "Do you always creep up behind people like that?"

She expected some smart-ass answer of either the joking-menacing or the hey-baby variety. But Ash just frowned at her moodily. "No. What are you doing out here?"

Mary-Lynnette's heart skipped several beats. But she heard her own voice answering flatly, "I'm starwatching. I do it every night. You might want to make a note of that for the thought police."

He looked at her, then at the station wagon. "Starwatching?"

"Of course. From that hill." She gestured.

Now he was looking at the camera looped around her neck. "No telescope," he commented skeptically. "Or is that what's in the car?"

Mary-Lynnette realized she was still holding the keys, ready to open the back of the wagon. "I didn't bring a telescope tonight." She went around to the passenger side of the car, unlocked the door, and reached in to pull out her binoculars. "You don't need a telescope to starwatch. You can see plenty with these."

"Oh, really?"

"Yes, *really*." Now, that was a mistake, Mary-Lynnette thought, suddenly grimly amused. Acting as if you don't believe me . . . just you *wait*.

"You want to see light from four million years ago?" she said. Then, without waiting for him to answer: "Okay. Face east." She rotated a finger at him. "Here, take the binoculars. Look at that line of fir trees on the horizon. Now pan up . . ." She gave him directions, rapping them out like a drill sergeant. "Now do you see a bright disk with a kind of smudge all around it?"

"Um. Yeah."

"That's Andromeda. Another *galaxy*. But if you tried to look at it through a telescope, you couldn't see it all at once. Looking through a telescope is like looking at the sky through a soda straw. That's all the field of view you get."

"All right. Okay. Point taken." He started to lower the binoculars. "Look, could we suspend the starwatching for just a minute? I wanted to talk to you. . . ."

"Want to see the center of *our* galaxy?" Mary-Lynnette interrupted. "Turn south."

She did everything but physically make him turn. She didn't dare touch him. There was so much adrenaline racing through her system already—if she made contact she might go supercritical and explode.

"Turn," she said. He shut his eyes briefly, then turned, bringing the binoculars up again.

"You have to look in the constellation Sagittarius." She rattled off instructions. "See that? That's where the center of the Milky Way is. Where all the star clouds are."

"How nice."

"Yes, it is nice. Okay, now go up and east—you should be able to find a little dim sort of glow. . . ."

"The pink one?"

She gave him a quick look. "Yeah, the pink one. Most people don't see that. That's the Trifid Nebula."

"What are those dark lines in it?"

Mary-Lynnette stopped dead.

She forgot her drill sergeant manner. She stepped back. She stared at him. She could feel her breath coming quicker.

He lowered the binoculars and looked at her. "Something wrong?"

"They're dark nebulae. Lanes of dust in front of the hot gas. But . . . you can't see them."

"I just did."

"No. No. You can't *see* those. It's not possible, not with binoculars. Even if you had nine millimeter pupils . . ." She pulled the flashlight out of her pocket and trained it full in his face.

"Hey!" He jerked back, eyes squeezing shut, hand over them. "That *hurt*!"

But Mary-Lynnette had already seen. She couldn't tell what color his eyes were right now, because the colored parts, the irises, were reduced to almost invisible rings. His eye was *all* pupil. Like a cat's at maximum dilation.

Oh, my God . . . the things he must be able to *see.* Eighth-magnitude stars, maybe ninth-magnitude stars. Imagine that, seeing a Mag 9 star with your naked eye. To see colors in the star clouds—hot hydrogen glowing pink, oxygen shining green-blue. To see thousands more stars cluttering the sky . . .

"Quick," she said urgently. "How many stars do you see in the sky right now?"

"I can't see *anything*," he said in a muffled voice, hand still over his eyes. "I'm *blind*."

"No, I mean *seriously*," Mary-Lynnette said. And she caught his arm.

It was a stupid thing to do. She wasn't thinking. But when she touched his skin, it was like completing a current. Shock swept over her. Ash dropped his hand and looked at her.

For just a second they were face-to-face, gazes locked. Something like lightning trembled between them. Then Mary-Lynnette pulled away.

I can't *take* any more of this. Oh, God, why am I even standing here talking to him? I've got enough ahead of me tonight. I've got a *body* to find.

"That's it for the astronomy lesson," she said, holding out a hand for the binoculars. Her voice was just slightly unsteady. "I'm going up the hill now."

She didn't ask where *he* was going. She didn't care, as long as it was away.

He hesitated an instant before giving her the binoculars, and when he did he made sure not to touch her.

Fine, Mary-Lynnette thought. We both feel the same.

"Goodbye."

"Bye," he said limply. He started to walk away. Stopped, his head lowered. "What I wanted to say . . ."

"Well?"

Without turning, he said in a flat and perfectly composed voice, "Stay away from my sisters, okay?"

Mary-Lynnette was thunderstruck. So outraged and full of disbelief that she couldn't find words. Then she thought: Wait, maybe he knows they're killers and he's trying to protect me. Like Jeremy.

Around the sudden constriction in her throat she managed to say, "Why?"

He shook his drooping head. "I just don't think you'd be a very good influence on them. They're kind of impressionable, and I don't want them getting any ideas."

Mary-Lynnette deflated. I should have known, she thought. She said, sweetly and evenly, "Ash? Get bent and die."

CHAPTER 8

She waited another hour after he set off down the road, heading east—doing what, she had no idea. There was nothing that way except two creeks and lots of trees. And her house. She hoped he was going to try to walk into town, and that he didn't realize how far it was.

All right, he's gone, now forget about him. You've got a job to do, remember? A slightly dangerous one. And he's not involved. I don't believe he knows anything about what happened to Mrs. B.

She got the shovel and started down the road west. As she walked she found that she was able to put Ash out of her mind completely. Because all she could think of was what was waiting ahead.

I'm not scared to do it; I'm not scared; I'm not scared. . . . Of *course* I'm scared.

But being scared was good; it would make her careful.

She would do this job quickly and quietly. In through the gap in the hedge, a little fast work with the shovel, and out again before anybody saw her.

She tried not to picture what she was going to find with that shovel if she was right.

She approached Burdock Farm cautiously, going north and then doubling back southeast to come in through the back property. The farmland had gone wild here, taken over by poison oak, beargrass, and dodder, besides the inevitable blackberry bushes and gorse. Tan oaks and chinquapins were moving in. Sometime soon these pastures would be forest.

I'm not sure I believe I'm doing this, Mary-Lynnette thought as she reached the hedge that surrounded the garden. But the strange thing was that she *did* believe it. She was going to vandalize a neighbor's property and probably look at a dead body—and she was surprisingly cool about it. Scared but not panicked. Maybe there was more hidden inside her than she realized.

I may not be who I've always thought I am.

The garden was dark and fragrant. It wasn't the irises and daffodils Mrs. B. had planted; it wasn't the fireweed and bleeding heart that were growing wild. It was the goats.

Mary-Lynnette stuck to the perimeter of the hedge, eyes on the tall upright silhouette of the farmhouse. There were only two windows lit.

Please don't let them see me and please don't let me make a noise.

Still looking at the house, she walked slowly, taking careful baby steps to the place where the earth was disturbed. The first couple of swipes with the shovel hardly moved the soil.

Okay. Put a little conviction in it. And don't watch the house; there's no point. If they look out, they're going to see you, and there's nothing you can do about it.

Just as she put her foot on the shovel, something went *hoosh* in the rhododendrons behind her.

Crouched over her shovel, Mary-Lynnette froze.

Stop worrying, she told herself. That's not the sisters. It's not Ash coming back. That's an animal.

She listened. A mournful *maaaa* came from the goat shed.

It wasn't anything. It was a rabbit. *Dig!*

She got out a spadeful of dirt—and then she heard it again.

Hoosh.

A snuffling sound. Then a rustling. Definitely an animal. But if it was a rabbit, it was an awfully loud one.

Who cares what it is? Mary-Lynnette told herself. There aren't any *dangerous* animals out here. And I'm not afraid of the dark. It's my natural habitat. I *love* the night.

But tonight, somehow, she felt differently. Maybe it was just the scene with Ash that had shaken her, made her feel confused and discontented. But just now she felt almost as if something was trying to tell her that the dark wasn't *any* human's natural habitat. That she wasn't built for it, with her weak eyes and her insensitive ears and dull nose. That she didn't belong.

Hoosh.

I may have rotten hearing, but I can hear *that* just fine. And it's big. Something big's sniffing around in the bushes.

What kind of big animal could be out here? It wasn't a deer; deer went *snort-wheeze.* It sounded larger than a coyote, taller. A bear?

Then she heard a different sound, the vigorous shaking of dry, leathery rhododendron leaves. In the dim light from the house she could *see* the branches churning as something tried to emerge.

It's coming out.

Mary-Lynnette clutched her shovel and ran. Not toward the gap in the hedge, not toward the house—they were both too dangerous. She ran to the goat shed.

I can defend myself in here—keep it out—hit it with the shovel. . . .

The problem was that she couldn't *see* from in here. There were two windows in the shed, but between the dirt on the glass and the darkness outside, Mary-Lynnette couldn't make out anything. She couldn't even see the goats, although she could hear them.

Don't turn on the penlight. It'll just give away your position.

Holding absolutely still, she strained to hear anything from outside.

Nothing.

Her nostrils were full of goat. The layers of oat straw

and decomposing droppings on the floor were smelly, and they kept the shed too warm. Her palms were sweating as she gripped the shovel.

I've never hit anybody . . . not since Mark and I were kids fighting . . . but, heck, I kicked a stranger this morning. . . .

She hoped the potential for violence would come out now when she needed it.

A goat nudged her shoulder. Mary-Lynnette shrugged it away. The other goat bleated suddenly and she bit her lip.

Oh, God—I heard something out there. The goat heard it, too.

She could taste her bitten lip. It was like sucking on a penny. Blood tasted like copper, which, she realized suddenly, tasted like fear.

Something opened the shed door.

What happened then was that Mary-Lynnette panicked.

Something unholy was after her. Something that sniffed like an animal but could open doors like a human. She couldn't see what it was—just a shadow of darkness against darkness. She didn't think of turning on the penlight—her only impulse was to smash out with the shovel *now*, to get It before It could get her. She was tingling with the instinct for pure, primordial violence.

Instead, she managed to hiss, "Who is it? Who's there?"

A familiar voice said, "I *knew* you were going to do this. I've been looking *everywhere* for you."

"Oh, *God*, Mark." Mary-Lynnette sagged against the wall of the shed, letting go of the shovel.

The goats were both bleating. Mary-Lynnette's ears were ringing. Mark shuffled farther in.

"Jeez, this place smells. What are you doing in here?"

"You *jerk*," Mary-Lynnette said. "I almost brained you!"

"You said you were forgetting all this crazy stuff. You lied to me."

"Mark, you don't . . . We can talk later. . . . Did you *hear* anything out there?" She was trying to gather her thoughts.

"Like what?" He was so calm. It made Mary-Lynnette feel vaguely foolish. Then his voice sharpened. "Like a yowling?"

"No. Like a snuffling." Mary-Lynnette's breath was slowing.

"I didn't hear anything. We'd better get out of here. What are we supposed to say if Jade comes out?"

Mary-Lynnette didn't know how to answer that. Mark was in a different world, a happy, shiny world where the worst that could happen tonight was embarrassment.

Finally she said, "Mark, listen to me. I'm your sister. I don't have any reason to lie to you, or play tricks on you, or put down somebody you like. And I don't just jump to conclusions; I don't imagine things. But I'm telling you, *absolutely seriously*, that there is something *weird* going on with these girls."

Mark opened his mouth, but she went on relentlessly. "So now there are only two things you can believe, and one is that

I'm completely out of my mind, and the other is that it's true. Do you *really* think I'm crazy?"

She was thinking of the past as she said it, of all the nights they'd held on to each other when their mother was sick, of the books she'd read out loud to him, of the times she'd put Band-Aids on his scrapes and extra cookies in his lunch. And somehow, even though it was dark, she could sense that Mark was remembering, too. They'd shared so much. They would always be connected.

Finally Mark said quietly, "You're not crazy."

"Thank you."

"But I don't know *what* to think. Jade wouldn't hurt anybody. I just *know* that. And since I met her . . ." He paused. "Mare, it's like now I know why I'm alive. She's different from any girl I've ever known. She's—she's so brave, and so funny, and so . . . *herself*."

And I thought it was the blond hair, Mary-Lynnette thought. Shows how shallow I am.

She was moved and surprised by the change in Mark—but mostly she was frightened. Frightened sick. Her cranky, cynical brother had found somebody to care about at last . . . and the girl was probably descended from Lucrezia Borgia.

And now, even though she couldn't see him, she could hear earnest appeal in his voice. "Mare, can't we just go home?"

Mary-Lynnette felt sicker.

"Mark—"

She broke off and they both snapped their heads to look at the shed window. Outside a light had gone on.

"Shut the door," Mary-Lynnette hissed, in a tone that made Mark close the door to the shed instantly.

"And be *quiet*," she added, grabbing his arm and pulling him next to the wall. She looked cautiously out the window.

Rowan came out of the back door first, followed by Jade, followed by Kestrel. Kestrel had a shovel.

Oh. My. God.

"What's happening?" Mark said, trying to get a look. Mary-Lynnette clamped a hand over his mouth.

What was happening was that the girls were digging up the garden again.

She didn't see anything wrapped in garbage bags this time. So what were they doing? Destroying the evidence? Were they going to take it into the house and burn it, chop it up?

Her heart was pounding madly.

Mark had scooted up and was looking out. Mary-Lynnette heard him take a breath—and then choke. Maybe he was trying to think of an innocent explanation for this. She squeezed his shoulder.

They both watched as the girls took turns with the shovel. Mary-Lynnette was impressed all over again at how strong they were. Jade looked so fragile.

Every time one of the sisters glanced around the garden,

Mary-Lynnette's heart skipped a beat. Don't see us, don't hear us, don't catch us, she thought.

When a respectable mound of dirt had piled up, Rowan and Kestrel reached into the hole. They lifted out the long garbage-bagged bundle Mary-Lynnette had seen before. It seemed to be stiff—and surprisingly light.

For the first time, Mary-Lynnette wondered if it was *too* light to be a body. Or too stiff . . . how long did rigor mortis last?

Mark's breathing was irregular, almost wheezing.

The girls were carrying the bundle to the gap in the hedge.

Mark cursed.

Mary-Lynnette's brain was racing. She hissed, "Mark, stay here. I'm going to follow them—"

"I'm going with you!"

"You have to tell Dad if anything happens to me—"

"I'm going *with* you."

There wasn't time to argue. And something inside Mary-Lynnette was glad to have Mark's strength to back her.

She gasped, "Come on, then. And don't make a sound."

She was worried they might have already lost the sisters—it was such a dark night. But when she and Mark squeezed through the gap in the rhododendron bushes, she saw a light ahead. A tiny, bobbing white light. The sisters were using a flashlight.

Keep quiet, move carefully. Mary-Lynnette didn't dare

say it out loud to Mark, but she kept thinking it over and over, like a mantra. Her whole consciousness was fixed on the little shaft of light that was leading them, like a comet's tail in the darkness.

The light took them south, into a stand of Douglas fir. It wasn't long before they were walking into forest.

Where are they *going*? Mary-Lynnette thought. She could feel fine tremors in her muscles as she tried to move as quickly as possible without making a sound. They were lucky—the floor of this forest was carpeted with needles from Douglas fir and Ponderosa pine. The needles were fragrant and slightly damp and they muffled footsteps. Mary-Lynnette could hardly hear Mark walking behind her except when he hurt himself.

They went on for what seemed like forever. It was pitch dark and Mary-Lynnette very quickly lost any sense of where they were. Or how they were going to get back.

Oh, God, I was crazy to do this—and to bring Mark along, too. We're out in the middle of the woods with three crazy girls. . . .

The light had stopped.

Mary-Lynnette stopped, holding out an arm that Mark immediately ran into. She was staring at the light, trying to make sure it really wasn't moving away.

No. It was steady. It was pointed at the ground.

"Let's get closer," Mark whispered, putting his lips against Mary-Lynnette's ear. She nodded and began to creep toward the light, as slowly and silently as she knew how. Every few steps she paused and stood absolutely still, waiting to see if the light was going to turn her way.

It didn't. She got down and crawled the last ten feet to the edge of the clearing where the girls had stopped. Once there, she had a good view of what they were doing.

Digging. Kestrel had shoveled the pine needles aside and was working on a hole.

Mary-Lynnette felt Mark crawl up beside her, crushing sword fern and woodfern. She could feel his chest heaving. She knew he saw what she saw.

I'm so sorry. Oh, Mark, I'm so sorry.

There was no way to deny it now. Mary-Lynnette *knew*. She didn't even need to look in the bag.

How am I going to find this place again? When I bring the sheriff back, how am I going to remember it? It's like a maze in one of those computer fantasy games—Mixed Evergreen Forest in every direction, and nothing to distinguish any bit of it from any other bit.

She chewed her lip. The bed of moist needles she was lying on was soft and springy—actually comfortable. They could wait here for a long time, until the sisters left, and then mark the trees somehow. Take photographs. Tie their socks to branches.

In the clearing the flashlight beam showed a hand putting down the shovel. Then Rowan and Kestrel lifted the garbage-bagged bundle—Jade must be holding the flashlight, Mary-Lynnette thought—and lowered it into the hole.

Good. Now cover it up and leave.

The beam showed Rowan bending to pick up the shovel again. She began quickly covering the hole with dirt. Mary-Lynnette was happy. Over soon, she thought, and let out a soft breath of relief.

And in that instant everything in the clearing changed.

The flashlight beam swung wildly. Mary-Lynnette flattened herself, feeling her eyes widen. She could see a silhouette against the light—golden hair haloed around the face. Kestrel. Kestrel was standing, facing Mark and Mary-Lynnette, her body tense and still. Listening. Listening.

Mary-Lynnette lay absolutely motionless, mouth open, trying to breathe without making a sound. There were things crawling in the soft, springy needle bed under her. Centipedes and millipedes. She didn't dare move even when she felt something tickle across her back under her shirt.

Her own ears rang from listening. But the forest was silent . . . eerily silent. All Mary-Lynnette could hear was her own heart pounding wildly in her chest—although it *felt* as if it were in her throat, too. It made her head bob with its rhythm.

She was afraid.

And it wasn't just fear. It was something she couldn't remember experiencing since she was nine or ten. *Ghost fear.*

The fear of something you're not even sure exists.

Somehow, watching Kestrel's silhouette in the dark woods, Mary-Lynnette was afraid of monsters. She had a terrible, terrible feeling.

Oh, please—I shouldn't have brought Mark here.

It was then that she realized that Mark's breathing was making a noise. Just a faint sound, not a whistling, more like a cat purring. It was the sound he'd made as a kid when his lungs were bad.

Kestrel stiffened, her head turning, as if to locate a noise.

Oh, Mark, *no.* Don't breathe. *Hold your breath—*

Everything happened very fast.

Kestrel sprang forward. Mary-Lynnette saw her silhouette come running and jumping with unbelievable speed. *Too* fast—nobody moves *that* fast . . . nobody human. . . .

What are these girls?

Her vision came in flashes, as if she were under a strobe light. Kestrel jumping. Dark trees all around. A moth caught in the beam.

Kestrel coming down.

Protect Mark . . .

A deer. Kestrel was coming down on a deer. Mary-Lynnette's mind was filled with jumbled, careening images. Images that didn't make sense. She had a wild thought that it wasn't Kestrel at all, but one of those raptor dinosaurs she'd seen at the movies. Because Kestrel moved like that.

Or maybe it wasn't a deer—but Mary-Lynnette could see the white at its throat, as pure as a lace ruffle at the throat of a young girl. She could see its liquid black eyes.

The deer screamed.

Disbelief.

I can't be seeing this, . . .

The deer was on the ground, delicate legs thrashing. And Kestrel was tangled with it. Her face buried in the white of its throat. Her arms around it.

The deer screamed again. Wrenched violently. Seemed to be having convulsions.

The flashlight beam was all over the place. Then it dropped. At the very edge of the light, Mary-Lynnette could see two other figures join Kestrel. They were all holding the deer. There was one last spasm and it stopped fighting. Everything went still. Mary-Lynnette could see Jade's hair, so fine that individual strands caught the light against the background of darkness.

In the silent clearing the three figures cradled the deer. Huddling over it. Shoulders moving rhythmically. Mary-Lynnette couldn't see exactly what they were doing, but the general scene was familiar. She'd seen it on dozens of nature documentaries. About wild dogs or lionesses or wolves. The pack had hunted and now it was feeding.

I have always tried . . . to be a very good observer. And now, I have to believe my own eyes. . . .

Beside her, Mark's breath was sobbing.

Oh, God, let me get him out of here. Please just let us get out.

It was as if she'd been suddenly released from paralysis. Her lip was bleeding again—she must have bitten down on it while she was watching the deer. Copperbloodfear filled her mouth.

"Come on," she gasped almost soundlessly, wiggling backward. Twigs and needles raked her stomach as her T-shirt rode up. She grabbed Mark's arm. "Come on!"

Instead, Mark lurched to his feet.

"Mark!" She wrenched herself to her knees and tried to drag him down.

He pulled away. He took a step toward the clearing.

No—

"Jade!"

He was heading for the clearing.

No, Mary-Lynnette thought again, and then she was moving after him. They were caught now, and it really didn't matter what he did. But she wanted to be with him.

"Jade!" Mark said and he grabbed the flashlight. He turned it directly on the little huddle at the edge of the clearing. Three faces turned toward him.

Mary-Lynnette's mind reeled. It was one thing to guess what the girls were doing; it was another thing to *see* it. Those three beautiful faces, white in the flashlight beam . . . with what looked like smeared lipstick on their mouths and chins. Cardinal red, thimbleberry color.

But it wasn't lipstick or burst thimbleberries. It was blood, and the deer's white neck was stained with it.

Eating the deer; they're really *eating the deer*; oh, God, they're really doing it. . . .

Some part of her mind—the part that had absorbed horror movies—expected the three girls to hiss and cringe away from the light. To block it out with bloodstained hands while making savage faces.

It didn't happen. There were no animal noises, no demon voices, no contortions.

Instead, as Mary-Lynnette stood frozen in an agony of horror, and Mark stood trying to get a normal breath, Jade straightened up.

And said, "What are you guys doing out here?"

In a puzzled, vaguely annoyed voice. The way you would speak to some boy who keeps following you everywhere and asking you for a date.

Mary-Lynnette felt her mind spinning off.

There was a long silence. Then Rowan and Kestrel stood up. Mark was breathing heavily, moving the flashlight from one of the girls to another, but always coming back to Jade.

"What are *you* doing out here; that's the question!" he said raggedly. The flashlight whipped to the hole, then back to the girls. "What are you *doing*?"

"I asked you first," Jade said, frowning. If it had just been her, Mary-Lynnette would have started to wonder if things were so awful after all. If maybe they weren't in terrible danger.

But Rowan and Kestrel were looking at each other, and then at Mark and Mary-Lynnette. And their expressions made Mary-Lynnette's throat close.

"You shouldn't have followed us," Rowan said. She looked grave and sad.

"They shouldn't have been *able* to," Kestrel said. She looked grim.

"It's because they smell like goats," Jade said.

"What are you doing?" Mark shouted again, almost sobbing. Mary-Lynnette wanted to reach for him, but she couldn't move.

Jade wiped her mouth with the back of her hand. "Well, can't you *tell*?" She turned to her sisters. "Now what are we supposed to do?"

There was a silence. Then Kestrel said, "We don't have a choice. We have to kill them."

CHAPTER 9

Mary-Lynnette's hearing had gone funny. She heard Kestrel's words like a character remembering a phrase in a bad movie. Kill them, kill them, kill them.

Mark laughed in a very strange way.

This is going to be really rotten for him, Mary-Lynnette thought, curiously dispassionate. I mean, if we were going to *live* through this, which we're not, it would be really rotten for him. He was already afraid of girls, and sort of pessimistic about life in general.

"Why don't we all sit down?" Rowan said with a stifled sigh. "We've got to figure this out."

Mark threw back his head and gave another short bark of a laugh.

"Why not?" he said. "Let's all sit down, why not?"

They're fast as whippets, Mary-Lynnette thought. If we run now, they'll catch us. But if we sit, and they get comfortable, and I distract them—or hit them with something . . .

"Sit!" she ordered Mark briskly. Rowan and Kestrel moved away from the deer and sat. Jade stood with her hands on her hips for a moment, then sat, too.

Sitting, Mark was still acting punch-drunk. He waved the flashlight around. "You girls are *something else*. You girls are really—"

"We're vampires," Jade said sharply.

"Yeah." Mark laughed quietly to himself. "Yeah," he said again.

Mary-Lynnette took the flashlight away from him. She wanted control of it. And it was heavy plastic and metal. It was a weapon.

And while one layer of her mind was thinking: *Shine the light in their eyes at just the right moment and then hit one of them;* another part was thinking: *She means they're people who* think *they're vampires; people with that weird disease that makes them anemic;* and one final part was saying: *You might as well face it; they're real.*

Mary-Lynnette's world view had been knocked right out of the ballpark.

"Don't you just *hate* that," Mark was saying. "You meet a girl and she seems pretty nice and you tell all your friends and then before you know it she turns out to be a *vampire*. Don't you just hate it when that happens?"

Oh, God, he's hysterical, Mary-Lynnette realized.

She grabbed his shoulder and hissed in his ear, "Get a grip, *now.*"

"I don't see what the point is in talking to them, Rowan," Kestrel was saying. "You know what we have to do."

And Rowan was rubbing her forehead. "I was thinking we might influence them," she said in an undertone.

"You know why that won't work." Kestrel's voice was soft and flat.

"Why?" Jade said sharply.

"They followed us for a reason," Rowan said tiredly. She nodded toward the hole. "So they've been suspicious for a while—for how long?" She looked at Mary-Lynnette.

"I saw you dig the hole Tuesday night," Mary-Lynnette said. *She* nodded toward the hole. "Is that your aunt in there?"

There was a brief silence and Rowan looked self-conscious. Then she inclined her head slightly. Gracefully.

"Oh, hell," Mark said. His eyes were shut and his head was rolling on his neck. "*Oh*, hell. They've got Mrs. B. in a bag."

"Two days," Rowan said to Jade. "They've suspected for two whole days. And we can't remove memories that are interlaced with other things for that long. We'd never know if we got them all."

"Well, we could just take *everything* for the last two days," Jade said.

Kestrel snorted. "And have two more people wandering around with lost time?"

Mary-Lynnette's mind went click. "Todd Akers and Vic Kimble," she said. "You did something to give them amnesia. I *knew* there had to be a connection."

"There's no other choice for us," Kestrel said quietly to Rowan. "And you know it as well as I do."

She's not being malicious, Mary-Lynnette realized. Just practical. If a lioness or a wolf or a falcon could talk, it would say the same thing. "We have to either kill or die; it's as simple as that."

Despite herself, Mary-Lynnette felt something like fascination—and respect.

Mark had his eyes open now. And Rowan was looking sad, so sad. It's awful, her expression said, but somebody here is going to have to get hurt.

Rowan bowed her head, then lifted it to face Mary-Lynnette directly. Their eyes met, held. After a moment Rowan's face changed slightly and she nodded.

Mary-Lynnette knew that in that instant they were communicating without words. Each recognizing the other as an alpha female who was willing to fight and die for her kin.

Meaning they were both big sisters.

Yes, somebody's going to get hurt, Mary-Lynnette thought. You threaten my family, I fight back.

She knew Rowan understood. Rowan was going to really hate killing her. . . .

"No," a voice said passionately, and Mary-Lynnette realized

it was Jade. And the next second Jade was on her feet, hands clenched, words erupting like a steam boiler exploding. "No, you *can't* kill Mark. I won't *let* you."

Rowan said, "Jade, I know this is hard—"

Kestrel said, "Jade, don't be a wimp—"

Jade was trembling, body tensed like a cat ready to fight. Her voice was louder than either of them. "You just can't do it! I think—I think—"

"Jade—"

"I think he's my soulmate!"

Dead silence.

Then Rowan groaned. "Oh, dear . . ."

Kestrel said, "Oh, *sure.*"

They were both looking at Jade. Focused on her. Mary-Lynnette thought, *Now.*

She swung the flashlight viciously at Kestrel wanting to take her out first, betting that Rowan would stay behind if Kestrel were hurt. But the swing never connected. Mark threw himself in front of her, slamming into her arm.

"Don't hurt Jade!"

Then everything was just a mad tangle. Arms, legs, grasping fingers, kicking feet. Jade and Mark both yelling for it to stop. Mary-Lynnette felt the flashlight wrenched out of her hand. She found long hair, got hold of it, yanked. Someone kicked her, and pain blossomed in her ribs.

Then she felt herself being dragged backward. Mark was

holding her, pulling her away from the fight. Jade was lying on top of Kestrel and clutching at Rowan.

Everybody was panting. Mark was almost crying.

"We just can't do this," he said. "This is terrible. This is all wrong."

Meanwhile Jade was snarling, "He's my soulmate, okay? *Okay?* I can't do anything with him *dead*!"

"He's not your soulmate, idiot," Kestrel said in a somewhat muffled voice. She was facedown on the carpet of needles. "When you're soulmates, it hits you like lightning, and you know that's the one person in the world you were meant to be with. You don't *think* you're soulmates; you just know it's your destiny whether you like it or not."

Somewhere, deep in Mary-Lynnette's brain, something stirred in alarm. But she had more urgent things to worry about.

"Mark, get out of here," she said breathlessly. "Run!"

Mark didn't even ease his grip. "Why do we have to be enemies?"

"Mark, they're *killers*. You can't justify that. They killed their own aunt."

Three faces turned toward her, startled. A half-full moon had risen above the trees, and Mary-Lynnette could see them clearly.

"We did *not*!" Jade said indignantly.

"What made you think that?" Rowan asked.

Mary-Lynnette felt her mouth hang open. "Because you *buried* her, for God's sake!"

"Yes, but we found her dead."

"Somebody staked her," Kestrel said, brushing pine needles out of her golden hair. "Probably a vampire hunter. I don't suppose you'd know anything about *that*."

Mark gulped. "Staked her—with a stake?"

"Well, with a picket from the fence," Kestrel said.

"She was already dead?" Mary-Lynnette said to Rowan. "But then why on earth did you bury her in the backyard?"

"It would have been disrespectful to leave her in the cellar."

"But why didn't you have her taken to a *cemetery*?"

Rowan looked dismayed.

Jade said, "Um, you haven't seen Aunt Opal."

"She's not looking so good," Kestrel said. "Kind of hard and stiff. You might say mummified."

"It's what happens to us," Rowan said almost apologetically.

Mary-Lynnette slumped back against Mark, trying to get her new world view into place. Everything was whirling.

"So . . . you were just trying to hide her. But . . . you *did* do something to Todd Akers and Vic Kim—"

"They *attacked* us," Jade interrupted. "They were thinking very bad things and they pinched our arms."

"They—?" Mary-Lynnette sat up suddenly. All at once she understood. "Oh, my God. Those jerks!"

Why hadn't she thought of that? Todd and Vic—last year there had been rumors about them jumping some girl from Westgrove. So they'd tried it on these girls, and . . .

Mary-Lynnette gasped and then snorted with half-inhaled laughter. "Oh, no. Oh, I hope you got them good. . . ."

"We just bit them a little," Rowan said.

"I wish I'd been there to *see* it."

She was laughing. Rowan was smiling. Kestrel was grinning barbarically. And suddenly Mary-Lynnette knew that they weren't going to fight anymore.

Everybody took a deep breath and sat back and looked at one another.

They do look different from normal humans, Mary-Lynnette thought, staring at them in the moonlight. It's so obvious once you know.

They were inhumanly beautiful, of course. Rowan with her soft chestnut hair and sweet face; Kestrel with her feral sleekness and golden eyes; Jade with her delicate features and her hair like starshine. Like the Three Graces, only fiercer.

"Okay," Rowan said softly. "We seem to have a situation here. Now we've got to figure something out."

"We won't tell on you," Mark said. He and Jade were gazing at each other.

"We've got Romeo and Juliet on our hands here is what we've got," Mary-Lynnette said to Rowan.

But Kestrel was speaking to Rowan, too. "No matter *what*

they promise, how do we know we can believe them?"

Rowan considered, eyes roving around the clearing. Then she let out a long breath and nodded.

"There's only one way," she said. "Blood-tie."

Kestrel's eyebrows flew up. "Oh, really?"

"What is it?" Mary-Lynnette asked.

"A blood-tie?" Rowan looked helpless. "Well, it's a kinship ceremony, you know." When Mary-Lynnette just looked at her, she went on: "It makes our families related. It's like, one of our ancestors did it with a family of witches."

Witches, Mary-Lynnette thought. Oh . . . gosh. So witches are real, too. I wonder how many other things are real that I don't know about?

"Vampires don't usually get along with witches," Rowan was saying. "And Hunter Redfern—that's our ancestor—had a real blood feud going with them back in the sixteen hundreds."

"But then he couldn't have kids," Jade said gleefully. "And he needed a witch to help or the whole Redfern family would end with him. So he had to apologize and do a kinship ceremony. And then he had all *daughters*. Ha ha."

Mary-Lynnette blinked. Ha ha?

"So, you see, we're part witch. All the Redferns are," Rowan was explaining in her gentle teaching voice.

"Our father used to say that's why we're so disobedient," Jade said. "Because it's in our *genes.* Because in witch families, *women* are in charge."

Mary-Lynnette began to like witches. "Ha ha," she said. Mark gave her a skittish sideways look.

"The point is that we could do a ceremony like that now," Rowan said. "It would make us family forever. We couldn't betray each other."

"No problem," Mark said, still looking at Jade.

"Fine with *me*," Jade said, and gave him a quick, fierce smile.

But Mary-Lynnette was thinking. It was a serious thing Rowan was talking about. You couldn't do something like this on a whim. It was worse than adopting a puppy; it was more like getting married. It was a *lifetime* responsibility. And even if these girls didn't kill humans, they killed animals. With their teeth.

But so did people. And not always for food. Was it worse to drink deer blood than to make baby cows into boots?

Besides, strange as it seemed, she felt close to the three sisters already. In the last couple of minutes she'd established more of a relationship with Rowan than she ever had with any girl at school. Fascination and respect had turned into a weird kind of instinctive trust.

And beside *that*, what other real choice was there?

Mary-Lynnette looked at Mark, and then at Rowan. She nodded slowly.

"Okay."

Rowan turned to Kestrel.

"So I'm supposed to decide, am I?" Kestrel said.

"We can't do it without you," Rowan said. "You know that."

Kestrel looked away. Her golden eyes were narrowed. In the moonlight her profile was absolutely perfect against the darkness of trees. "It would mean we could never go home again. Make ourselves kin to vermin? That's what *they'd* say."

"Who's vermin?" Mark said, jolted out of his communion with Jade.

Nobody answered. Jade said, with odd dignity, "I can't go home, anyway. I'm in love with an Outsider. And I'm going to tell him about the Night World. So I'm dead no matter what." Mark was opening his mouth—to protest that Jade shouldn't take such a risk for *him*, Mary-Lynnette thought—when Jade added absently, "And so is he, of course."

Mark shut his mouth.

Rowan said, "Kestrel, we've come too far to go back."

Kestrel stared at the forest for another minute or so. Then suddenly she turned back to the others, laughing. There was something wild in her eyes.

"All right, let's go the whole way," she said. "Tell them everything. Break every rule. We might as well."

Mary-Lynnette felt a twinge. She hoped she wasn't going to regret this. But what she said was "Just how do we do this—ceremony?"

"Exchange blood. I've never done it before, but it's simple."

"It might be a *little* bit strange, though," Jade said, "because you'll be a little bit vampires afterward."

"A little bit *what*?" Mary-Lynnette said, her voice rising in spite of her.

"Just a *little* bit." Jade was measuring out tiny bits of air between her index finger and thumb. "A drop."

Kestrel cast a look skyward. "It'll go away in a few days," she said heavily, which was what Mary-Lynnette wanted to know.

"As long as you don't get yourself bitten by a vampire again in the meantime," Rowan added. "Otherwise, it's perfectly safe. Honestly."

Mary-Lynnette and Mark exchanged glances. Not to discuss things, they'd gone beyond that now. Just to brace themselves. Then Mary-Lynnette took a deep breath and flicked a bit of fern off her knee.

"Okay," she said, feeling lightheaded but determined. "We're ready."

CHAPTER 10

It felt like a jellyfish sting.

Mary-Lynnette kept her eyes shut and her face turned away as Rowan bit into her neck. She was thinking of the way the deer had screamed. But the pain wasn't so bad. It went away almost immediately.

She could feel warmth at her neck as the blood flowed, and, after a minute, a slight dizziness. A weakness. But the most interesting thing was that all at once she seemed to have a new sense. She could sense Rowan's *mind.* It was like seeing, but without eyes—and using different wavelengths than visual light. Rowan's mind—her presence—was warm red, like glowing embers in a campfire. It was also fuzzy and rounded like a ball of hot gas floating in space.

Is this what psychics mean when they talk about people having an aura?

Then Rowan pulled back, and it was over. The new sense disappeared.

Mary-Lynnette's fingers went automatically to her neck. She felt wetness there. A little tenderness.

"Don't fool with it," Rowan said, brushing at her lips with her thumb. "It'll go away in just a minute."

Mary-Lynnette blinked, feeling languid. She looked over at Mark, who was being released by Kestrel. He looked okay, if a little dazed. She smiled at him and he raised his eyebrows and shook his head slightly.

I wonder what *his* mind looks like, Mary-Lynnette thought. Then she said, startled, "What are you doing?"

Rowan had picked up a twig and was testing its end for sharpness.

"Every species has some substance that's harmful to it," she said. "Silver for werewolves, iron for witches . . . and wood for vampires. It's the only thing out here that will cut our skin," she added.

"I didn't mean that. I meant *why*," Mary-Lynnette said, but she knew why already. She watched redness bead in the wake of the twig as Rowan drew it across her wrist.

Exchange blood, Rowan had said.

Mary-Lynnette gulped. She didn't look at Mark and Kestrel.

I'll do it first and then he'll see it's not so bad, she told herself. I can do this, I can do this. . . . It's so we can stay *alive.*

Rowan was looking at her, offering her wrist.

Copperbloodfear, Mary-Lynnette thought, feeling queasy.

She shut her eyes and put her mouth to Rowan's wrist.

Warmth. Well-being. And a taste not like copper, but like something rich and strange. Later, she'd always grope for ways to describe it, but she could only think of things like: well, a little bit like the way vanilla bean smells, and a little bit like the way silk feels, and a little bit like the way a waterfall looks. It was faintly sweet.

Afterward, she felt as if she could run up mountains.

"*Oh*, boy," Mark said, sounding giddy. "If you could bottle that stuff, you'd make millions."

"It's been thought of before," Kestrel said coolly. "Humans hunting us for our blood."

"Talk later," Rowan said firmly. "Blood-tie now."

Kestrel's mind was gold. With brilliant knifelike edges sending glitters in every direction.

"Okay, Jade," Rowan said. "Mark. Enough, you guys. Let go of each other now."

Mary-Lynnette saw that she was physically pulling Mark and Jade apart. Mark was wearing a silly smile, and Mary-Lynnette felt the tiniest stab of envy. What would it be like to see the mind of somebody you were in love with?

Jade's mind was silver and lacy, an intricate filigreed sphere like a Christmas ornament. And by the time Mary-Lynnette sat back from drinking Jade's blood, she felt light-headed and sparkling. As if she had a mountain stream in her veins.

"All right," Rowan said. "Now we share the same blood." She held out a hand, and Jade and Kestrel did the same. Mary-Lynnette glanced at Mark, then they each reached out, all their hands meeting like spokes in a wheel.

"We promise to be kin to you, to protect and defend you always," Rowan said. She nodded to Mary-Lynnette.

"We promise to be kin to you," Mary-Lynnette repeated slowly. "To protect and defend you always."

"That's it," Rowan said simply. "We're family."

Jade said, "Let's go *home*."

They had to finish burying Aunt Opal first. Mary-Lynnette watched as Rowan scattered pine needles over the grave.

"You inherit our blood feuds, too," Kestrel told Mary-Lynnette pleasantly. "Meaning you have to help us find out who killed her."

"I've been trying to do that all along."

They left the deer where it was. Rowan said, "There are already lots of scavengers around here. It won't be wasted."

Yep, that's life, Mary-Lynnette thought as they left the clearing. She glanced behind her—and for just an instant she thought she saw a shadow there and a glint of greenish-orange eyes at her own eye level. It was much too big for a coyote.

She opened her mouth to tell the others . . . and the shadow was gone.

Did I imagine that? I think my eyes are going funny. Everything seems too bright.

All her senses seemed changed—sharpened. It made it easier to get out of the woods than it had been getting in. Mark and Jade didn't walk hand in hand—that would have been impractical—but Jade looked back at him frequently. And when they got to rough spots, they helped each other.

"You're happy, aren't you?" Mary-Lynnette said softly when she found herself beside Mark.

He gave a startled, sheepish grin, white in the moonlight. "Yeah. I guess I am." After a minute he said, "It's like—I don't know how to describe it, but it's like I belong with Jade. She really *sees* me. I mean, not the outside stuff. She sees me *inside*, and she likes me. Nobody else has ever done that . . . except you."

"I'm happy for you."

"Listen," he said. "I think we should start looking around for you. There are lots of guys around here—"

Mary-Lynnette snorted. "Mark. If I want to meet a guy, I'll meet a guy. I don't need any help."

He gave the sheepish grin again. "Sorry."

But Mary-Lynnette was thinking. Of *course* she'd like to find somebody who would accept her completely, who would share everything with her. That was everybody's dream. But for how many people did it come true?

And there *weren't* lots of guys around here. . . .

She found herself thinking of Jeremy Lovett again. His clear brown eyes . . .

But she couldn't hold the picture. It kept dissolving—to her horror—into eyes that flashed blue and gold and gray, depending on the way they caught the light.

Oh, God, *no.* Ash was the last person who would understand her. And she didn't want to share a bus seat with him, much less her life.

"What I want to know is who *made* you guys vampires," Mark said. They were sitting on oversize, overstuffed Victorian furniture in the living room at Burdock Farm. Rowan had a fire going in the fireplace. "Was it the old lady? Your aunt?"

"It wasn't anybody," Jade said, looking affronted. "We're not *made* vampires. We're the lamia." She pronounced it LAY-mee-uh.

Mark looked at her sideways. "Uh-huh. And what's that?"

"It's *us.* It's vampires that can have babies, and eat, and drink, and get old if we let ourselves, and live in families. The *best* kind of vampires."

"It's a race of vampires, basically," Kestrel said. "Look, there are two different kinds of vampires, okay? The kind who start out as humans and are changed when a vampire bites them, and the kind that are *born* vampires. That's the kind we are. Our line goes back—well, let's say a long way."

"The longest," Jade broke in again. "We're Redferns; we go back to prehistoric times."

Mary-Lynnette blinked. "But *you three* don't go back that far, do you?" she said nervously.

Rowan stifled a laugh. "I'm nineteen; Kestrel's seventeen; Jade is sixteen. We haven't stopped aging yet."

Kestrel was looking at Mary-Lynnette. "How old did our aunt look to you?"

"Um, around seventy, seventy-five, I guess."

"When we last saw her she looked maybe forty," Kestrel said. "That was ten years ago, when she left our island."

"But she'd actually been alive for seventy-four years at that point," Rowan said. "That's what happens to us—if we stop holding off the aging process, it all catches up at once."

"Which if you've been alive for five or six hundred years can be quite interesting," Kestrel said dryly.

Mary-Lynnette said, "So this island where you come from—is that the Night World?"

Rowan looked startled. "Oh, no, it's just a safe town. You know, a place where our people all live without any humans. Hunter Redfern founded it back in the sixteenth century so we'd have somewhere safe to live."

"The only problem," Kestrel said, golden eyes glinting, "is that people there are still *doing* things the way they did in the sixteenth century. And they made a rule that nobody could *leave*—except for some of the men and boys that they trusted completely."

Like Ash, I guess, Mary-Lynnette thought. She was about to say this, but Rowan was speaking again.

"So that's why we ran away. We didn't want to have to get married when our father told us to. We wanted to see the human world. We wanted—"

"To eat *junk* food," Jade caroled. "And read magazines and wear pants and watch TV."

"When Aunt Opal left the island, she didn't tell anybody where she was going—except me," Rowan said. "She told me she was going to this little town called Briar Creek where her husband's family had built a house a hundred and fifty years ago."

Mary-Lynnette ran her fingers through the silky tassels of a forest-green pillow. "Okay, but—where *is* the Night World, then?"

"Oh . . . it's not a place. . . ." Rowan looked uncertain. "This is—it's kind of hard to tell you, actually," she said. "You're not even supposed to know it *exists.* The two very first laws of the Night World are that you never let a human find out about it . . . and that you never fall in love with a human."

"And Jade's breaking both this minute," Kestrel murmured.

Jade just looked pleased.

"And the penalty for both is death—for everybody involved," Rowan said. "But . . . you're family. Here goes." She took a steadying breath. "The Night World is a sort of secret society. Not just of vampires. Of witches and werewolves and shapeshifters, too. All the different kinds of Night People. We're everywhere."

Everywhere? Mary-Lynnette thought. It was an unnerving idea—but an interesting one. So there was a whole world out there she'd never known about—a place to explore, as alien as the Andromeda galaxy.

Mark didn't seem too disturbed by the thought of vampires everywhere. He was grinning at Jade, leaning with one elbow on the arm of the dark green couch. "So, can you read *minds*? Can you read my mind *right now*?"

"Soulmates can read each other's minds without even trying," Jade told Mark firmly.

Soulmates . . . Mary-Lynnette wanted to get on to a different subject. She felt uncomfortable, tingly.

"I wish you'd stop saying that. What you have is much better than being soulmates," Rowan was telling Jade. "With love you get to find out about a person first. Being soulmates is involuntary—you don't even have to *like* the person when you meet them. They may be completely wrong for you in every way—wrong species, wrong temperament, wrong age. But you know you'll never be completely happy again without them."

More and more tingly. Mary-Lynnette had to say something. "And what if that happened to you—if you found somebody and you were soulmates with them and you didn't want to be?" she asked Rowan. She realized that her voice was strange—thick. "Isn't there any way you could—get rid of it?"

There was a pause. Mary-Lynnette saw everyone turn to look at her.

"I've never heard of one," Rowan said slowly. Her brown eyes were searching Mary-Lynnette's. "But I guess you could ask a witch . . . if you had that problem."

Mary-Lynnette swallowed. Rowan's eyes were gentle and friendly—and Mary-Lynnette felt a very strong need to talk to *someone*, someone who would understand.

"Rowan—"

She didn't get any further. Rowan, Kestrel, and Jade all looked suddenly toward the front door—like cats who have heard something their humans can't. An instant later, though, Mary-Lynnette heard it, too. The sound of feet on the front porch—*tap, tap, tap*—as quick as that. And then a thud.

"Hey, somebody's *out* there," Jade said, and before Mark could stop her, she was up and heading for the door.

CHAPTER 11

"Jade—wait a minute!" Mark said.

Jade, of course, didn't wait even a second. But she lost time undoing the bolts on the front door, and Mary-Lynnette could hear the quick *tap, tap, tap* of somebody running away.

Jade threw the door open, darted out onto the porch—and screamed. Mary-Lynnette crowded forward and saw that Jade had put her foot into one of the holes where the porch was missing a board. Everybody who didn't know the place did that. But that wasn't what had made her scream.

It was the goat.

"Oh, God," Mark said. "Oh, God—who would do that?"

Mary-Lynnette took one look and felt a burning in her chest and arms—a painful, bad feeling. Her lungs seemed to contract and her breath was forced out. Her vision blurred.

"Let's get it inside," Rowan said. "Jade, are you all right?"

Jade was taking in ragged, whooping breaths. She sounded the way Mary-Lynnette felt. Mark leaned over to help pull her out of the hole.

Rowan and Kestrel were lifting the goat by its legs. Mary-Lynnette was backing into the house, teeth clamped on her already-bitten lip. The taste of copper was like a blood clot in her mouth.

They put the goat on an old-fashioned patterned rug in the entrance to the living room. Jade's whooping breaths turned into gasping sobs.

"That's Ethyl," Mary-Lynnette said. She felt like sobbing too.

She knelt beside Ethyl. The goat was pure white, with a sweet face and a broad forehead. Mary-Lynnette reached out to touch one hoof gently. She'd helped Mrs. B. trim that hoof with pruning shears.

"She's dead," Kestrel said. "You can't hurt her." Mary-Lynnette looked up quickly. Kestrel's face was composed and distant. Shock rippled under Mary-Lynnette's skin.

"Let's take them out," Rowan said.

"The hide's ruined already," Kestrel said.

"Kestrel, please—"

Mary-Lynnette stood. "Kestrel, *shut up*!"

There was a pause. To Mary-Lynnette's astonishment, the pause went on. Kestrel stayed shut up.

Mary-Lynnette and Rowan began to pull the little wooden stakes out of the goat's body.

Some were as small as toothpicks. Others were longer than Mary-Lynnette's finger and thicker than a shish kebab skewer, with a dull point at one end. Somebody *strong* did this, Mary-Lynnette thought. Strong enough to punch splinters of wood through goat hide.

Over and over again. Ethyl was pierced everywhere. Hundreds of times. She looked like a porcupine.

"There wasn't much bleeding," Rowan said softly. "That means she was dead when it was done. And look here." She gently touched Ethyl's neck. The white coat was crimson there—just like the deer, Mary-Lynnette thought.

"Somebody either cut her throat or bit it," Rowan said. "So it was probably quick for her and she bled out. Not like . . ."

"What?" Mary-Lynnette said.

Rowan hesitated. She looked up at Jade. Jade sniffled and wiped her nose on Mark's shoulder.

Rowan looked back at Mary-Lynnette. "Not like Uncle Hodge." She looked back down and carefully loosened another stake, adding it to the pile they were accumulating. "You see, they killed Uncle Hodge this way, the Elders did. Only he was alive when they did it."

For a moment Mary-Lynnette couldn't speak. Then she said, *"Why?"*

Rowan pulled out two more stakes, her face controlled and intent. "For telling a human about the Night World."

Mary-Lynnette sat back on her heels and looked at Mark.

Mark sat down on the floor, bringing Jade with him.

"That's why Aunt Opal left the island," Rowan said.

"And now somebody's staked Aunt Opal," Kestrel said. "And somebody's killed a goat in the same way Uncle Hodge was killed."

"But *who*?" Mary-Lynnette said.

Rowan shook her head. "Somebody who knows about vampires."

Mark's blue eyes looked darker than usual and a little glazed. "You were talking before about a vampire hunter."

"That gets my vote," Kestrel said.

"Okay, so who around here is a vampire hunter? *What's* a vampire hunter?"

"That's the problem," Rowan said. "I don't know how you could tell who is one. I'm not even sure I *believe* in vampire hunters."

"They're supposed to be humans who've found out about the Night World," Jade said, pushing tears out of her eyes with her palms. "And they can't get other people to believe them—or maybe they don't want other people to know. So they hunt us. You know, trying to kill us one by one. They're supposed to know as much about the Night World as Night People do."

"You mean, like knowing how your uncle was executed," Mary-Lynnette said.

"Yes, but that's not much of a secret," Rowan said. "I

mean, you wouldn't have to actually know about Uncle Hodge to think of it—it's the traditional method of execution among the lamia. There aren't many things besides staking and burning that will kill a vampire."

Mary-Lynnette thought about this. It didn't get them very far. Who would want to kill an old lady and a goat?

"Rowan? Why did your aunt have goats? I mean, I always thought it was for the milk, but . . ."

"It was for the blood, I'm sure," Rowan said calmly. "If she looked as old as you said, she probably couldn't get out into the woods to hunt."

Mary-Lynnette looked at the goat again, trying to find other clues, trying to be a good observer: detached, methodical. When her eyes got to Ethyl's muzzle, she blinked and leaned forward.

"I—there's something in her mouth."

"Please tell me you're joking," Mark said.

Mary-Lynnette just waved a hand at him. "I can't—I need something to . . . hang on a sec." She ran into the kitchen and opened a drawer. She snagged a richly decorated sterling silver knife and ran back to the living room.

"Okay," she grunted as she pried Ethyl's teeth farther open. There *was* something in there—something like a flower, but black. She worked it out with her fingers.

"Silence of the Goats," Mark muttered.

Mary-Lynnette ignored him, turning the disintegrating

thing over in her hands. "It looks like an iris—but it's spray-painted black."

Jade and Rowan exchanged grim glances. "Well—this has *something* to do with the Night World," Rowan said. "If we weren't sure of that before, we are now. Black flowers are the symbols of the Night World."

Mary-Lynnette put the sodden iris down. "Symbols, like . . . ?"

"We wear them to identify ourselves to each other. You know, on rings or pins or clothes or things like that. Each species has its own kind of flower, and then there are other flowers that mean you belong to a certain club or family. Witches use black dahlias, werewolves use black foxglove; made vampires use black roses . . ."

"And there's a chain of clubs called the Black Iris," Kestrel said, coming to stand by the others. "I know because Ash belongs to one."

"*Ash* . . ." Jade said, staring at Kestrel with wide green eyes.

Mary-Lynnette sat frozen. Something was tugging insistently at the corner of her consciousness. Something about a black design. . . .

"Oh, God," she said. "Oh, God—I know somebody who wears a ring with a black flower on it."

Everyone looked at her.

"Who?" Mark said, at the same time as Rowan said it. Mary-Lynnette didn't know which of them looked more surprised.

Mary-Lynnette struggled with herself for a minute.

"It's Jeremy Lovett," she said finally. Not too steadily.

Mark made a face. "That oddball. He lives by himself in a trailer in the woods, and last summer . . ." Mark's voice died out. His jaw dropped, and when he spoke again, it was more slowly. "And last summer they found a body right out near there."

"Can you tell?" Mary-Lynnette asked Rowan quietly. "If somebody's a Night Person?"

"Well . . ." Rowan looked dismayed. "Well—not for sure. If somebody was experienced at shielding their mind . . . Well, we *might* be able to startle them into revealing something. But otherwise, no. Not for *certain.*"

Mark leaned back. "Oh, terrific. Well, I think Jeremy would make a great Night Person. Actually, so would Vic Kimble and Todd Akers."

"Todd," Jade said. "Now, wait a minute." She picked up one of the toothpicks that had been embedded in the goat and stared at it.

Rowan was looking at Mary-Lynnette. "No matter what, we should go and see your friend Jeremy. He'll probably turn out to be completely innocent—sometimes a human gets hold of one of our rings or pins, and then things get *really* confusing. Especially if they wander into one of our clubs. . . ."

Mary-Lynnette wasn't so sure. She had a terrible, terrible

sick feeling. The way Jeremy kept to himself, the way he always seemed to be an outsider at school—even his untamed good looks and his easy way of moving . . . No, it all seemed to lead to one conclusion. She had solved the mystery of Jeremy Lovett at last, and it was *not* a happy ending.

Kestrel said, "Okay, fine; we can go check this Jeremy guy out. But what about Ash?"

"What about Ash?" Rowan said. The last stake was out. She gently turned one side of the rug over the body of the goat, like a shroud.

"Well, don't you see? It's his club flower. So maybe somebody from his club did it."

"Um, I know I'm starting to sound like a broken record," Mark said. "But I don't know what you're talking about. Who's Ash?"

The three sisters looked at him. Mary-Lynnette looked away. After so many missed opportunities, it was going to sound extremely peculiar when she casually mentioned that, oh, yes, she'd met Ash. Twice. But she didn't have a choice anymore. She had to tell.

"He's our brother," Kestrel was saying.

"He's crazy," Jade said.

"He's the only one from our family who might know that we're here in Briar Creek," Rowan said. "He found me giving a letter to Crane Linden to smuggle off the island. But I don't *think* he noticed Aunt Opal's address on it. He's not much good at noticing things that aren't about him."

"You can say that again," Jade said. "All Ash thinks about is Ash. He's completely self-centered."

"All he does is chase girls and party," Kestrel said, with one of those smiles that made Mary-Lynnette wonder if she really disapproved. "And hunt."

"He doesn't like humans," Jade said. "If he didn't like chasing human girls and playing with them, he'd probably be planning to *wipe out* all the humans and take over the world."

"Sounds like a great guy," Mark said.

"Well, he's sort of conservative," Rowan said. "Politically, I mean. Personally, he's—"

"Loose," Kestrel suggested, eyebrows up.

"To put it mildly," Jade agreed. "There's only one thing he wants when he goes after human girls—besides their cars, I mean."

Mary-Lynnette's heart was pounding. With every second that passed it was getting harder to speak up. And every time she took a breath, somebody else started talking.

"So, wait—you think *he* did all this stuff?" Mark asked.

"I wouldn't put it past him," Kestrel said.

Jade nodded vigorously.

"But his own *aunt*," Mark said.

"He'd do it if he thought the honor of the family was involved," Kestrel said.

"Yes, well, there's one problem with all that," Rowan said tightly. "Ash isn't *here.* He's in California."

"No, he's not," Ash said casually, from the back of the living room.

CHAPTER 12

What happened then was interesting. Mary-Lynnette got to see the sisters do all the things she'd missed earlier in the clearing. All the hissing and the clawed fingers. Just like the movies.

Except that when a vampire hissed, it sounded *real.* Like a cat, not like a person imitating a cat. All three girls jumped up and stood ready to fight.

There wasn't any weird grimacing. But Jade and Kestrel were showing teeth that were long and beautifully curved, coming to delicate feline points that indented the lower lip.

And something else. Their eyes changed. Jade's silvery-green eyes went even more silvery. Kestrel's golden eyes looked jewel-yellow, like a hawk's. Even Rowan's eyes had a dark light in them.

"Oh, boy," Mark whispered. He was standing beside Jade, staring from her to Ash.

Ash said, "Hi."

Don't look at him, Mary-Lynnette told herself. Her heart was pounding wildly and her knees were trembling. The attraction of particle to antiparticle, she thought, remembering a line from last year's physics class. But there was another, shorter name for it, and no matter what she said to herself, she couldn't keep it out of her mind.

Soulmates.

Oh, God, I really don't want this. Please, *please,* I didn't ask for this. I want to discover a supernova and study mini-quasars at the Gamma Ray Observatory. I want to be the one who solves the mystery of where all the dark matter in the universe is.

I don't want this.

It should have happened to someone like Bunny Marten, someone who spent time *longing* for romance. The only thing Mary-Lynnette longed for was somebody to understand . . .

. . . *to understand the night with you,* a distant part of her mind whispered.

And instead here she was, stuck with a guy whose own sisters were terrified of him.

It was true. That was why they were standing poised to fight, making threatening noises. Even *Kestrel* was afraid of him.

The moment Mary-Lynnette realized that, anger washed out the trembling dismay inside her. Whatever she felt about Ash, she wasn't afraid of him.

"Don't you ever *knock*?" she said and walked toward him. *Strode* toward him.

She had to hand it to her new family. Both Jade and Kestrel tried to grab her and keep her from getting close to their brother. Protecting her. Mary-Lynnette shook them off.

Ash eyed her warily.

"Oh. You," he said. Unenthusiastically.

"What are you doing here?"

"It's my uncle's house."

"It's your aunt's house and you weren't invited."

Ash looked at his sisters. Mary-Lynnette could just see little wheels turning in his head. Had they already told about the Night World or not? Of course, if they hadn't, their behavior should be giving somebody a clue. Most human girls didn't hiss.

Ash held one finger up. "Okay. Now, listen—"

Mary-Lynnette kicked him in the shins. She knew it was inappropriate, she knew it was uncalled-for, but she couldn't stop herself. She just *had* to.

"Oh, for God's sake," Ash said, hopping backward. "Are you *crazy*?"

"Yes, she is," Mark said, abandoning Jade and hurrying forward to take Mary-Lynnette's arm. "Everybody knows she's crazy. She can't help it." He backed up, pulling. He was looking at Mary-Lynnette as if she'd taken all her clothes off and started to dance the mambo.

So were Kestrel and Jade. Their eyes had gone ordinary, their teeth retracted. They'd never seen anyone treat their brother quite this way. And to have a *human* doing it . . .

If the girls had superhuman strength, Ash was undoubtedly even stronger. He could probably flatten Mary-Lynnette with one blow.

She *still* couldn't help it. She wasn't afraid of him, only of herself and the stupid floating feeling in her stomach. The way her legs wanted to fold under her.

"Will somebody just tell her not to do that anymore?" Ash was saying.

Kestrel and Jade looked sideways at Mary-Lynnette. Mary-Lynnette shrugged at them, her breath coming quickly.

She saw that Rowan was looking at her, too, but not in the same dumbfounded way. Rowan looked worried and surprised and sorry.

"You've met," she said.

"I should have told you," Mary-Lynnette said. "He came to our house. He was asking my stepmother about you and your friends—saying that he needed to approve them because he was head of the family."

All three girls looked at Ash with narrowed eyes.

"So you *have* been around," Kestrel said. "For how long?"

Rowan said quietly, "What are you really doing here?"

Ash let go of his shin. "Can we all sit down and talk about this like reasonable people?"

Everyone looked at Mary-Lynnette. She took a deep, calming breath. She still felt as if her entire skin was electrified, but her heart was slowing down. "Yes," she said and worked at looking normal so they'd know her temporary insanity was over.

As he helped her to the couch, Mark whispered, "I have to tell you, I've never seen you act so immature before. I'm proud of you."

Even big sisters have to have some off time, Mary-Lynnette thought. She patted him vaguely and sat, feeling tired.

Ash settled in a plush-covered chair. Rowan and Kestrel sat beside Mary-Lynnette. Mark and Jade shared an ottoman.

"All right," Ash said. "Now can we first introduce ourselves? I presume that's your brother."

"Mark," Mary-Lynnette said. "Mark, that's Ash."

Mark nodded. He and Jade were holding hands. Mary-Lynnette saw Ash's eyes drop to their intertwined fingers. She couldn't tell anything from his expression.

"Okay. Now." Ash looked at Rowan. "I'm here to take you back home, where everyone misses you violently."

Jade breathed, "Give me a break."

Kestrel said, "What if we don't want to be taken?" and showed her teeth briefly. Mary-Lynnette didn't find that strange. What she found strange was that Ash didn't return the smile. He didn't look lazy or sardonic or smug right then. He looked like somebody who wants to get a job over with.

Rowan said, "We can't go home, Ash." Her breathing was slightly irregular, but her chin was high.

"Well, you have to come home. Because otherwise there are going to be some fairly drastic consequences."

"We knew that when we left," Jade said, with as little emotion as Rowan. Her chin was high, too.

"Well, I don't think you've really thought it *through*." Ash's voice had an edge.

"We'd rather die than go back," Jade said.

Kestrel glanced at her quickly, one eyebrow raised.

"Oh, well, fine, I'll just make a note of that," Ash said tightly. Then his expression darkened. He looked more determined than Mary-Lynnette would have thought he *could* look. Not in the least like a big blond cat. Like a lanky, elegant pale tiger.

"Now, listen," he said. "There are a few small things that you don't understand, and I don't have any time to play games. So how about we send your little friends home and then we can all have a family talk."

Mary-Lynnette's hands clenched into fists.

Mark clutched at Jade, who pushed him away slightly with her elbow. She was frowning. "I think maybe you'd better," she said.

"I'm not going to leave you."

Rowan bit her lip. "Mark . . ."

"I'm not *going*. Don't try to protect me. He's not stupid;

sooner or later he's going to find out that we know about the Night World."

Rowan drew in her breath involuntarily. Kestrel's expression never changed, but her muscles tensed as if for a fight. Jade's eyes went silver. Mary-Lynnette sat very still.

They all looked at Ash. Ash looked heavenward.

"I know you know," he said with deadly patience. "I'm trying to get you out, you poor sap, before I find out how *much* you know."

The sisters stared. Mary-Lynnette opened her mouth and then shut it again.

"I thought you didn't like humans," Mark said.

"I don't; I hate them," Ash said with brittle cheer.

"Then why would you want to cut me a break?"

"Because if I kill you, I have to kill your sister," Ash informed him, with a smile that would have fit in perfectly at the Mad Hatter's tea party.

"So what; she kicked you."

Ash stopped tossing answers back like footballs. "Yeah, well, I may change my mind any minute."

"No, *wait*," Jade said. She was sitting with legs folded under her, staring at her brother fiercely. "This is just too weird. Why would you care what happens to a human?"

Ash didn't say anything. He looked at the fireplace bitterly.

It was Rowan who said softly, "Because they're soulmates."

An instant of silence, then everybody started talking explosively.

"They're what? You mean, like what Jade and I are?"

"Oh, Ash, this is rich. I just wish our father were here to see this."

"It is *not my fault*," Mary-Lynnette said. She found everyone turning toward her, and realized that her eyes were full.

Rowan leaned across Kestrel to put her hand on Mary-Lynnette's arm.

"You mean it's really true?" Mark said, looking from Mary-Lynnette to Ash.

"It's true. I guess. I don't know what it's supposed to be like," Mary-Lynnette said, concentrating on making the tears go away.

"It's true," Ash said moodily. "It doesn't mean we're going to *do* anything about it."

"Oh, you've got *that* right," Mary-Lynnette said. She was glad to be angry again.

"So let's all just pick up our toys and go home," Ash said in the general direction of his sisters. "We'll forget all about this; we'll just agree that it never happened."

Rowan was watching him, shaking her head slightly. There were tears in her eyes, but she was smiling.

"I never thought I'd hear you say something like that," she said. "You've changed so much—I can't believe it."

"I can't believe it, either," Ash said bleakly. "Maybe it's a dream."

"But you have to admit now that humans aren't vermin. You couldn't be soulmates with vermin."

"Yes. Fine. Humans are terrific. We all agree; now let's go home."

"When we were kids, you were like this," Rowan said. "Before you started acting like you were better than everyone. I always knew a lot of that was just show. To hide how scared you were. And I always knew you didn't really believe a lot of the horrible stuff you said. Somewhere inside, you're still that nice little kid, Ash."

Ash produced his first really *flashing* smile of the evening. "Don't bet on it."

Mary-Lynnette had listened to all this feeling shakier and shakier. To conceal it, she said to Rowan, "I don't think your aunt thought so."

Ash sat up. "Hey, where is the old hag, anyway? I need to have a talk with her before we leave."

This silence seemed endless.

"Ash . . . don't you know?" Rowan said.

"Of course he knows. Ten to one, he *did* it," Kestrel said.

"What is it that I'm supposed to know?" Ash said, with every sign of being about to lose his patience.

"Your aunt's dead," Mark told him.

"Somebody staked her," Jade added.

Ash looked around the room. His expression said he suspected it was a practical joke. Oh, God, Mary-Lynnette thought numbly, when he's startled and bewildered like that he looks so young. Vulnerable. Almost human.

"Somebody . . . murdered . . . Aunt Opal. That's what you're telling me?"

"Are you telling *us* that you don't know?" Kestrel asked. "What have you been *doing* all night, Ash?"

"Banging my head against a rock," Ash said. "Then looking for you. When I walked in you were talking about me."

"And you didn't run across any livestock tonight? Any—let's say—goats?"

Ash gave her a long, incredulous look. "I fed, if that's what you're asking. Not on a goat. *What* does this have to do with Aunt Opal?"

"I think we'd better show him," Rowan said.

She was the one who got up and lifted the fold of rug away from the goat. Ash walked around the couch to see what she was doing. Mary-Lynnette turned to watch his face.

He winced. But he controlled it quickly.

Rowan said quietly, "Look at what was in the goat's mouth."

Ash picked up the black flower gingerly. "An iris. So?"

"Been to your club recently?" Kestrel asked.

Ash gave her a weary look. "If *I* had done this, why would I sign it with an iris?"

"Maybe to tell us who did it."

"I don't have to kill goats to say things, you know. I *can* talk."

Kestrel looked unimpressed. "Maybe this way the message has a little more impact."

"Do I *look* like the kind of person who wastes time turning goats into pincushions?"

"No. No, I don't think you did this," Rowan said in her quiet way. "But *somebody* did—probably whoever killed Aunt Opal. We've been trying to figure out who."

"Well, who have we got for suspects?"

Everyone looked at Mary-Lynnette. She looked away.

"There's one who's pretty prime," Mark said. "His name's Jeremy Lovett. He's a real—"

"Quiet guy," Mary-Lynnette interrupted. If anyone was going to describe Jeremy, it was going to be her. "I've known him since elementary school, and I would never, *ever* have believed he could hurt anybody—especially an old lady and an animal."

"But his uncle was crazy," Mark said. "And I've heard things about his family—"

"Nobody *knows* anything about his family," Mary-Lynnette said. She felt as if she were struggling to keep her head above water, with barbells tied to her wrists and ankles. What was dragging her down wasn't Mark's suspicion—it was her own. The little voice in her head that was saying, "But he *seemed* like such a nice guy"—and which meant, of course, that he wasn't.

Ash was watching her with a brooding, intent expression. "What does this Jeremy look like?"

Something about the way he said it irritated Mary-Lynnette beyond belief. "What do you care?"

Ash blinked and shifted his gaze. He shrugged minimally and said with forced blandness, "Just curious."

"He's *very* handsome," Mary-Lynnette said. Good—a way to let out her anger and frustration. "And the thing is that he looks very intelligent and sensitive—it's not empty good looks. He's got hair that's sort of the color of Ponderosa pinecones and the most wonderful brown eyes. . . . He's thin and tan and a little bit taller than me, because I'm normally looking at his mouth. . . ."

Ash didn't look pleased. "I saw somebody vaguely like that at the gas station in town." He turned to Rowan. "You think he's some kind of outlaw vampire?"

"Obviously not a made vampire because Mary-Lynnette has watched him grow up," Rowan said. "I was thinking more that he might be renegade lamia. But there's not much use in trying to figure it out from here. Tomorrow we can go and *see* him, and then we'll know more. Right?"

Mark nodded. Jade nodded. Mary-Lynnette took a deep breath and nodded.

Ash nodded and said, "All right, I see why you can't go home until this is solved. So, we'll figure out who killed Aunt Opal, and then we'll take the appropriate action, and *then* we'll go home. Got it?"

His sisters exchanged glances. They didn't answer.

• • •

As she and Mark walked back to their house, Mary-Lynnette noticed that Sirius had lifted above the eastern horizon. It hung like a jewel, brighter than she had ever seen it before—much brighter. It seemed almost like a miniature sun, flashing with blue and gold and violet rays.

She thought the effect must be psychological, until she remembered that she'd exchanged blood with three vampires.

CHAPTER 13

Jade sat in the wing chair, holding Tiggy upside down on her lap, petting his stomach. He was purring but mad. She stared down into indignant, glowing green eyes.

"The other *goat*," Kestrel announced from the doorway, saying the word as if it were something not mentioned in polite society, "is just fine. So you can let the cat out."

Jade didn't think so. There was somebody crazy in Briar Creek, and she planned to keep Tiggy safe where she could see him.

"*We're* not going to have to feed on the goat, are we?" Kestrel asked Rowan dangerously.

"Of course not. Aunt Opal did because she was too old to hunt." Rowan looked preoccupied as she answered.

"I like hunting," Jade said. "It's even better than I thought it would be." But Rowan wasn't listening—she was biting her lip and staring into the distance. "Rowan, *what*?"

"I was thinking about the situation we're in. You and Mark, for one thing. I think we need to talk about that."

Jade felt reflexive alarm. Rowan was in one of her organizing moods—which meant you could blink and find that she'd rearranged all your bedroom furniture or that you were moving to Oregon. "Talk about what?" she said warily.

"About what you two are going to *do.* Is he going to stay human?"

"It's illegal to change him," Kestrel put in pointedly.

"Everything we've done this week is illegal," Rowan said. "And if they exchange blood again—well, it's only going to take a couple of times. Do you *want* him a vampire?" she asked Jade.

Jade hadn't thought about it. She thought Mark was nice the way he was. But maybe *he* would want to be one. "What are you going to do with yours?" she asked Ash, who was coming slowly downstairs.

"My what?" He looked sleepy and irritable.

"Your soulmate. Is Mary-Lynnette going to stay human?"

"That's the other thing I've been worrying about," Rowan said. "Have you thought at all, Ash?"

"I can't think at this hour in the morning. I don't have a brain yet."

"It's almost noon," Kestrel said scornfully.

"I don't care when it is. I'm still asleep." He wandered toward the kitchen. "And you don't need to worry," he added, looking back and sounding more awake. "Because I'm not doing *anything* with the girl and Jade's not doing anything with the brother. Because we're going *home*." He disappeared.

Jade's heart was beating hard. Ash might act frivolous, but she saw the ruthlessness underneath. She looked at Rowan.

"Is Mary-Lynnette *really* his soulmate?"

Rowan leaned back, her brown hair spreading like a waterfall on the green brocade of the couch. "I'm afraid so."

"But then how can he want to leave?"

"Well . . ." Rowan hesitated. "Soulmates don't always stay together. Sometimes it's too much—the fire and lightning and all that. Some people just can't stand it."

Maybe Mark and I aren't really soulmates, Jade thought. And maybe that's *good*. It sounds painful.

"Poor Mary-Lynnette," she said.

A clear voice sounded in her mind: *Why doesn't anybody say "Poor Ash"?*

"Poor Mary-Lynnette," Jade said again.

Ash reappeared. "Look," he said and sat down on one of the carved mahogany chairs. "We need to get things straight. It's not just a matter of *me* wanting you to come home. I'm not the only one who knows you're here."

Jade stiffened.

Kestrel said, almost pleasantly, "You *told* somebody?"

"I was staying with somebody when the family called to say you were missing. And he was there when I realized where you must have gone. He also happens to be an extremely powerful telepath. So just consider yourself lucky I convinced him to let me try to get you back."

Jade stared at him. She did consider herself lucky. She also considered it strange that Ash would go to such trouble for her and Rowan and Kestrel—for *anybody* besides Ash. Maybe she didn't know her brother as well as she thought.

Rowan said, very soberly, "Who was it?"

"Oh, nobody." Ash leaned back and looked moodily at the ceiling. "Just Quinn."

Jade flinched. Quinn . . . that *snake.* He had a heart like a glacier and he despised humans. He was the sort to take Night World law into his own hands if he didn't think it was being enforced properly.

"He's coming back on Monday to see if I've taken care of the situation," Ash said. "And if I haven't, we're all dead—you, me, *and* your little human buddies."

Rowan said, "So we've got until Monday to figure something out."

Kestrel said, "If he tries anything on *us*, he's in for a fight."

Jade squeezed Tiggy to make him growl.

Mary-Lynnette had been sleeping like a stone—but a stone with unusually vivid dreams. She dreamed about stars brighter than she'd ever seen and star clouds shimmering in colors like the northern lights. She dreamed about sending an astronomical telegram to Cambridge, Massachusetts, to register her claim for discovering a new supernova. About being the first to see it with her wonderful new eyes, eyes that—she saw in a mirror—were all pupil, like an owl's or a cat's. . . .

Then the dream changed and she *was* an owl, swooping down in a dizzying rush from a hollow Douglas fir. She seized a squirrel in her talons and felt a surge of simple joy. Killing felt so natural. All she had to do was be the best owl she could be, and grab food with her feet.

But then a shadow fell over her from somewhere above. And in the dream she felt a terrible sick realization—that even hunters could be hunted. And that something was after *her*. . . .

She woke up disoriented—not as to *where* she was, but as to *who* she was. Mary-Lynnette or a hunter being chased by something with white teeth in the moonlight? And even when she went downstairs, she couldn't shake off the sick feeling from her dream.

"Hi," Mark said. "Is that breakfast or lunch?"

"Both," Mary-Lynnette said, sitting down on the family room couch with her two granola bars.

Mark was watching her. "So," he said, "have you been thinking about it, too?"

Mary-Lynnette tore the wrapper off a granola bar with her teeth. "About what?"

"*You* know."

Mary-Lynnette did know. She glanced around to make sure Claudine wasn't in earshot. "*Don't* think about it."

"Why not?" When she didn't answer, he said, "Don't tell me you haven't been wondering what it would be like. To see better, hear better, be telepathic . . . and live *forever.* I mean, we could see the year three thousand. You know, the robot wars, colonizing other planets. . . . Come on, don't tell me you're not even a *little* curious."

All Mary-Lynnette could think of was a line from a Robert Service poem: *And the skies of night were alive with light, with a throbbing, thrilling flame. . . .*

"I'm curious," she said. "But there's no point in wondering. They do things we couldn't do—they *kill.*"

She put down her glass of milk as if she'd lost her appetite. She hadn't, though—and wasn't that the problem? She ought to be sick to her stomach at just the thought of killing, of drinking blood from a warm body.

Instead, she was scared. Of what was out there in the world—and of herself.

"It's *dangerous,*" she said aloud to Mark. "Don't you see? We've gotten mixed up in this Night World—and it's a place where bad things can happen. Not just bad like flunking a class. Bad like . . ."

. . . white teeth in the moonlight . . .

"Like getting killed *dead,*" Mary-Lynnette said. "And that's serious, Mark. It's not like the movies."

Mark was staring at her. "Yeah, but we knew that already." His tone said, *What's the big deal?*

And Mary-Lynnette couldn't explain. She stood up abruptly. "If we're going over there, we'd better get moving," she said. "It's almost one o'clock."

The sisters and Ash were waiting at Burdock Farm. "You and Mark can sit in the front with me," Mary-Lynnette told Jade, not looking at Ash. "But I don't think you'd better bring the cat."

"The cat goes," Jade said firmly, getting in. "Or I don't."

Mary-Lynnette put the car in gear and pulled out.

As they came in sight of the small cluster of buildings on Main Street, Mark said, "And there it is, downtown Briar Creek in all its glory. A typical Friday afternoon, with absolutely nobody on the streets."

He didn't say it with his usual bitterness. Mary-Lynnette glanced at him and saw that it was Jade he was talking to. And Jade was looking around with genuine interest, despite the cat's claws embedded in her neck.

"*Somebody's* on the streets," she said cheerfully. "It's that boy Vic. And that other one, Todd. And grown-ups."

Mary-Lynnette slowed as she passed the sheriff's office but didn't stop until she reached the gas station at the opposite corner. Then she got out and looked casually across the street.

Todd Akers was there with his father, the sheriff—and Vic Kimble was there with *his* father. Mr. Kimble had a farm east of town. They were all getting into the sheriff's car, and they all seemed very excited. Bunny Marten was standing on the sidewalk watching as they left.

Mary-Lynnette felt a twinge of fear. This is what it's like when you have a terrible secret, she thought. You worry about everything that happens, and wonder if it's got something to do with you, if it's going to get you caught.

"Hey, Bunny!" she called. "What's going on?"

Bunny looked back. "Oh, hi, Mare." She walked unhurriedly—Bunny never hurried—across the street. "How're you doing? They're just going to check out that horse thing."

"What horse thing?"

"Oh . . . didn't you hear?" Bunny was looking behind Mary-Lynnette now, at Mark and the four strangers who were getting out of the station wagon. Suddenly her blue eyes got rounder and she reached up to fluff her soft blond hair.

Now, I wonder who she's just seen, Mary-Lynnette thought ironically. Who *could* it be?

"Hi," Ash said.

"We didn't hear about the horse thing," Mary-Lynnette said, gently prompting.

"Oh . . . um, one of Mr. Kimble's horses cut his throat on barbed wire last night. That's what everybody was saying this morning. But just now Mr. Kimble came into town and said that he didn't think it was barbed wire after all. He thinks . . . somebody did it on purpose. Slashed its throat and left it to die."

She hunched her shoulders in a tiny shiver. Theatrically, Mary-Lynnette thought.

"You see?" Jade said. "That's why I'm keeping my eye on Tiggy."

Mary-Lynnette noticed Bunny eyeing Jade. "Thanks, Bun."

"I've got to get back to the store," Bunny said, but she didn't move. Now she was looking at Kestrel and Rowan.

"I'll walk you there," Ash said gallantly. With what, Mary-Lynnette thought, must be his usual putting-the-moves-on manner. "After all, we don't know what could be lurking around here."

"It's broad daylight," Kestrel said disgustedly, but Ash was already walking Bunny away. Mary-Lynnette decided she was glad to get rid of him.

"Who was that girl?" Rowan asked, and something in her voice was odd.

Mary-Lynnette glanced at her in surprise. "Bunny Marten. I know her from school. What's wrong?"

"She was staring at us," Rowan said softly.

"She was staring at Ash. Oh, and probably you three, too. You're new and you're pretty, so she's probably wondering which boys you'll take from her."

"I see." But Rowan still looked preoccupied.

"Rowan, what is it?"

"It's nothing. I'm sure it's nothing. It's just that she's got a lamia name."

"Bunny?"

"Well." Rowan smiled. "Lamia are traditionally named after natural things—gems and animals and flowers and trees. So 'Bunny' would be a lamia name—and isn't a marten a kind of weasel?"

Something was tugging at the edges of Mary-Lynnette's consciousness again. Something about Bunny . . . about Bunny and . . . wood . . .

It was gone. She couldn't remember. To Rowan she said, "But—can you sense something suspicious about her or anything? I mean, does she *seem* like one of you? Because otherwise I just can't see Bunny as a vampire. I'm sorry; I just *can't.*"

Rowan smiled. "No, I don't sense anything. And I'm sure you're right—humans can have names like ours, too. Sometimes it gets confusing."

For some bizarre reason Mary-Lynnette's mind was still on wood. "You know, I don't see why you name yourselves after trees. I thought wood was dangerous for you."

"It is—and that makes it powerful. Tree names are supposed to be some of the most powerful names we have."

Ash was coming out of the general store. Immediately Mary-Lynnette turned around and looked for Jeremy.

She didn't see him in the empty gas station, but she heard something—something she realized she'd been hearing for several minutes. Hammering.

"Come on, let's go around back," she said, already walking,

not waiting for Ash to reach them. Kestrel and Rowan went with her.

Jeremy was around back. He was hammering a long board across a broken window. There were shards of thick, greenish-tinted glass all over the ground. Light brown hair was falling in his eyes as he struggled to hold the board steady.

"What happened?" Mary-Lynnette said. She moved automatically to hold the right end of the board in place for him.

He glanced up at her, making a grimace of relief as he let go of the board. "Mary-Lynnette—thanks. Hang on a sec."

He reached into his pocket for nails and began driving them in with quick, sure blows of the hammer. Then he said, "I don't know what happened. Somebody broke it last night. Made a real mess."

"Last night seems to have been a busy night," Kestrel said dryly.

Jeremy glanced back at the voice. And then . . . his hands went still, poised with the hammer and nail. He was looking at Kestrel, and at Rowan beside her, looking a long time. At last he turned to Mary-Lynnette and said slowly, "You need more gas already?"

"Oh—no. No." I should have siphoned some out, Mary-Lynnette thought. Nancy Drew would definitely have thought of that. "I just—it's been knocking a lot—the engine—and I thought you could look at it—under the hood—since you didn't last time."

Incoherent and pathetic, she decided in the silence that followed. And Jeremy's clear brown eyes were still searching her face.

"Sure, Mary-Lynnette," he said—not sarcastically, but gently. "As soon as I get finished."

Oh, he *can't* be a vampire. And so what am I doing here, lying to him, suspecting him, when he's only ever been nice to me? He's the type to *help* old ladies, not kill them.

Sssssss.

She started as the feral hiss tore through the silence. It came from behind her, and for one horrible instant she thought it was Kestrel. Then she saw that Jade and Mark had rounded the corner, and that Tiggy was fighting like a baby leopard in Jade's arms. The kitten was spitting and clawing, black fur standing on end. Before Jade could get a better grip, he climbed up her shoulder and leaped, hitting the ground running.

"Tiggy!" Jade shrieked. She took off after him, silvery blond hair flying, agile as a kitten herself. Mark followed, ricocheting off Ash who was just coming around the corner himself. Ash was knocked into the gas station wall.

"Well, that was fun," Kestrel said.

But Mary-Lynnette wasn't really listening. Jeremy was staring at Ash—and his expression gave Mary-Lynnette cold chills.

And Ash was staring back with eyes as green as glacier ice. Their gazes were locked in something like instantaneous, instinctive hatred. Mary-Lynnette felt a quiver of fear for Jeremy—but Jeremy didn't seem afraid for himself. His muscles were tight and he looked ready to defend himself.

Then, deliberately, he turned away. Turned his back on Ash. He readjusted the board—and Mary-Lynnette did what she should have done in the beginning. She looked at his hand. The ring on his index finger glinted gold, and she could just make out the black design on the seal.

A tall cluster of bell-shaped flowers. Not an iris, not a dahlia, not a rose. No—there was only one flower Rowan had mentioned that this could possibly be. It grew wild around here and it was deadly poison.

Foxglove.

So now she knew.

Mary-Lynnette felt hot and sick. Her hand began to tremble on the board she was holding. She didn't want to move, but she couldn't stay here.

"I'm sorry—I have to get something—" The words came out in a painful gasp. She knew everyone was staring at her. She didn't care. She let go of the board and almost ran away.

She kept going until she was behind the boarded-up windows of the Gold Creek Hotel. Then she leaned against the wall and stared at the place where town ended and the wilderness began. Motes of dust danced in the sunlight, bright against a dark background of Douglas fir.

I'm so *stupid.* All the signs were there, right in front of my face. Why didn't I see before? I guess because I didn't *want* to. . . .

"Mary-Lynnette."

Mary-Lynnette turned toward the soft voice. She resisted the impulse to throw herself into Rowan's arms and bawl.

"I'll be okay in just a few minutes. Really. It's just a shock."

"Mary-Lynnette . . ."

"It's just—it's just that I've known him so long. It's not easy to picture him—you know. But I guess it just goes to show you. People are never what they seem."

"Mary-Lynnette—" Rowan stopped and shook her head. "Just what are you talking about?"

"*Him.* Jeremy. Of course." Mary-Lynnette took a breath. The air felt hot and chokingly dusty. "He did it. He really did it."

"Why do you think so?"

"*Why?* Because he's a *werewolf.*"

There was a pause and Mary-Lynnette suddenly felt embarrassed. She looked around to make sure nobody was in earshot and then said more quietly, "Isn't he?"

Rowan was looking at her curiously. "How did you know?"

"Well—you said black foxglove is for werewolves. And that's foxglove on his ring. How did *you* know?"

"I just sensed it. Vampire powers are weaker in sunlight, but Jeremy isn't trying to hide anything. He's right out there."

"He sure is," Mary-Lynnette said bitterly. "*I* should have

sensed it. I mean . . . he's the only person in town who was interested in the lunar eclipse. And the way he moves, and his eyes . . . and he lives at Mad Dog Creek, for God's sake. I mean, that land's been in his family for generations. *And*"—Mary-Lynnette gave a sudden convulsive sniffle—"people say they've seen the Sasquatch around there. A big hairy monster, half person and half beast. Now, what does *that* sound like?"

Rowan was standing quietly, her expression grave—but her lips were twitching. Mary-Lynnette's vision blurred and wetness spilled onto her cheeks.

"I'm sorry." Rowan put a hand on her arm. "I'm not laughing."

"I thought he was a nice guy," Mary-Lynnette said, turning away.

"I still think he is," Rowan said. "And actually, really, you know, it means he *didn't* do it."

"The fact that he's a nice guy?"

"The fact that he's a werewolf."

Mary-Lynnette turned back. *"What?"*

"You see," Rowan said, "werewolves are different. They're not like vampires. They can't drink a little blood from people and then stop without doing any real harm. They kill every time they hunt—because they have to *eat.*" Mary-Lynnette gulped, but Rowan went on serenely. "Sometimes they eat the whole animal, but they *always* eat the internal organs, the heart and liver. They have to do it, the same way that vampires need to drink blood."

"And that means . . ."

"He didn't kill Aunt Opal. Or the goat. They were both intact." Rowan sighed. "Look. Werewolves and vampires traditionally hate each other. They've been rivals forever, and lamia think of werewolves as sort of—lower class. But actually a lot of them are gentle. They only hunt to eat."

"Oh," Mary-Lynnette said hollowly. Shouldn't she be happier about this? "So the guy I thought was nice just has to eat the odd liver occasionally."

"Mary-Lynnette, you can't blame him. How can I explain? It's like this: Werewolves aren't people who sometimes turn into wolves. They're wolves who sometimes look like people."

"But they still kill," Mary-Lynnette said flatly.

"Yes, but only animals. The law is *very* strict about that. Otherwise humans catch on in no time. Vampires can disguise their work by making it look like a cut throat, but werewolf kills are unmistakable."

"Okay. Great." I should be more enthusiastic, Mary-Lynnette thought. But how could you ever really trust someone who was a wolf behind their eyes? You might admire them the way you admire a sleek and handsome predator, but trust them . . . no.

"Before we go back—we may have a problem," Rowan said. "If he realizes that you recognized his ring, he may know we've told you about—you know." She glanced around and lowered her voice. "The Night World."

Mary-Lynnette understood. "Oh, God."

"Yes. That means it's his duty to turn us all in. Or kill us himself."

"Oh, God."

"The thing is, I don't think he will. He likes you, Mary-Lynnette. A lot. I don't think he could bring himself to turn you in."

Mary-Lynnette felt herself flushing. "But then, that would get *him* in trouble, too, wouldn't it?"

"It could, if anybody ever finds out. We'd better go back and see what's going on. Maybe he *doesn't* realize you know. Maybe Kestrel and Ash have managed to bluff him."

CHAPTER 14

They walked back to the gas station quickly, their shoulders almost touching. Mary-Lynnette found comfort in Rowan's nearness, in her levelheadedness. She'd never had a friend before who was completely her equal, who found it as easy to take care of people as to be taken care of.

As they reached the gas station, they could see that the little group was now clustered around Mary-Lynnette's car. Jeremy was peering under the hood. Mark and Jade were back, hand in hand, but there was no sign of Tiggy. Kestrel was leaning against a gas pump, and Ash was talking to Jeremy.

"So the werewolf walks into the second doctor's office and he says, 'Doc, I think I have rabies.' And the doctor says . . ."

So much for bluffing him, Mary-Lynnette thought.

Rowan, eyes shut and shoulders tensed, said, "Ash, that

isn't funny." She opened her eyes. "I'm sorry," she said to Jeremy. "He doesn't mean it."

"He does, but it doesn't matter. I've heard worse." Jeremy bent over the engine again. He replaced a cap with careful, even twists. Then he looked up at Mary-Lynnette.

Mary-Lynnette didn't know what to say. What's the etiquette when you've just discovered that somebody's a werewolf? And that it may be their duty to eat you?

Her eyes filled. She was completely out of control today.

Jeremy looked away. He shook his head slightly. His mouth was bitter. "That's what I figured. I thought you'd react this way. Or I'd have told you myself a long time ago."

"You would?" Mary-Lynnette's vision cleared. "But—then *you* would have gotten in trouble. Right?"

Jeremy smiled faintly. "Well, we're not really sticklers for Night World law around here."

He said it in a normal tone of voice. Ash and the sisters looked around reflexively.

Mary-Lynnette said, "'We'?"

"My family. They first settled here because it was so far out of the way. A place where they wouldn't bother anybody, and nobody would bother them. Of course, they're all gone now. There's only me left."

He said it without self-pity, but Mary-Lynnette moved closer. "I'm sorry."

Jade moved in on the other side, silvery-green eyes wide.

"But that's why we came here, too! So nobody would bother us. We don't like the Night World, either."

Jeremy gave another faint smile—that smile that showed mostly in his eyes. "I know," he said to Jade. "You're related to Mrs. Burdock, aren't you?"

"She was our aunt," Kestrel said, her golden gaze fixed unwaveringly on him.

Jeremy's expression changed slightly. He turned around to look at Kestrel directly. "'Was'?"

"Yes, she met with a slight accident involving a stake," Ash said. "Funny how that happens sometimes. . . ."

Jeremy's expression changed again. He looked as if he were leaning against the car for support. "Who did it?" Then he glanced back at Ash, and Mary-Lynnette saw a gleam of teeth. "Wait—you think *I* did. Don't you?"

"It did cross our minds at one point," Ash said. "Actually, it seemed to keep crossing them. Back and forth. Maybe we should put in a crosswalk."

Mary-Lynnette said, "Ash, stop it."

"So you're saying you *didn't* do it," Mark said to Jeremy, at the same time as Rowan said, "Actually, Kestrel thinks it was a vampire hunter."

Her voice was soft, but once again, everybody looked around. The street was still deserted.

"There's no vampire hunter around here," Jeremy said flatly.

"Then there's a vampire," Jade said in an excited whisper.

"There *has* to be, because of the way Aunt Opal was killed. And the goat."

"The goat . . . ? No, don't even tell me. I don't want to know." Jeremy swung Mary-Lynnette's hood shut. He looked at her and said quickly, "Everything's fine in there. You should get the oil changed sometime." Then he turned to Rowan. "I'm sorry about your aunt. But if there *is* a vampire around here, it's somebody staying hidden. *Really* hidden. Same if it's a vampire hunter."

"We already figured that out," Kestrel said. Mary-Lynnette expected Ash to chime in, but Ash was staring across the street broodingly, his hands in his pockets, apparently having given up on the conversation for the moment.

"You haven't seen anything that could give you a clue?" Mary-Lynnette said. "We were going to look around town."

He met her eyes directly. "If I knew, I'd tell you." There was just the slightest emphasis on the last word. "If I could help you, I would."

"Well, come along for the ride. You can put your head out of the window," Ash said, returning to life.

That did it. Mary-Lynnette marched over, grabbed him by the arm, and said to the others, "Excuse us." She hauled him in a series of tugs to the back of the gas station. "You jerk!"

"Oh, look . . ."

"Shut up!" She jabbed a finger at his throat. It didn't matter that touching him set off electrical explosions. It just gave her

another reason to want to kill him. She found that the pink haze was a lot like anger when you kept shouting through it.

"You have to be the center of every drama, don't you? You have to be the center of attention, and act smart, and mouth off!"

"Ow," Ash said.

"Even if it means hurting other people. Even if it means hurting somebody who's only had rotten breaks all his life. Well, *not this time*."

"Ow . . ."

"Rowan said you guys think all werewolves are low class. And you know what that is? Where I come from, they call that prejudice. And humans have it, too, and *it is not a pretty picture.* It's about the most hateful thing in the world. I'm *ashamed* to even stand there while you spout it off." Mary-Lynnette realized she was crying. She also realized that Mark and Jade were peering around the edge of the gas station.

Ash was flat against the boarded-up window, arms up in a gesture of surrender. He looked at a loss for words—and ashamed. Good, Mary-Lynnette thought.

"Should you keep poking him that way?" Mark said tentatively. Mary-Lynnette could see Rowan and Kestrel behind him and Jade. They all looked alarmed.

"I can't be friends with anybody who's a bigot," she said to all of them. She gave Ash a jab for emphasis.

"*We're* not," Jade said virtuously. "*We* don't believe that stupid stuff."

"We really don't," Rowan said. "And Mary-Lynnette—our father is always yelling at Ash for visiting the wrong kind of people on the Outside. Belonging to a club that admits werewolves, having werewolves for friends. The Elders all say he's *too* liberal about that."

Oh. "Well, he's got a funny way of showing it," Mary-Lynnette said, deflating slightly.

"I just thought I'd mention that," Rowan said. "Now we'll leave you alone." She herded the others back toward the front of the station.

When they were gone, Ash said, "Can I move now, please?" He looked as if he was in a very bad mood.

Mary-Lynnette gave up. She felt tired, suddenly—tired and emotionally drained. Too much had happened in the last few days. And it *kept* happening, it never let up, and . . . well, she was tired, that's all.

"If you'd go away soon, it would be easier," she said, moving away from Ash. She could feel her head sag slightly.

"Mary-Lynnette . . ." There was something in Ash's voice that she'd never heard before. "Look—it's not exactly a matter of me *wanting* to go away. There's somebody else from the Night World coming on Monday. His name is Quinn. And if my sisters and I don't go back with him, the whole *town* is in trouble. If he thinks anything irregular is going on here . . . You don't know what the Night People can do."

Mary-Lynnette could hear her heart beating distinctly. She didn't turn back to look at Ash.

"They could wipe Briar Creek out. I mean it. They've *done* things like that, to preserve the secret. It's the only protection they have from your kind."

Mary-Lynnette said—not defiantly, but with simple conviction, "Your sisters aren't going to leave."

"Then the whole town's in trouble. There's a rogue werewolf, three renegade lamia, and a secret vampire killer wandering around somewhere—not to mention two humans who know about the Night World. This is a paranormal disaster area."

A long silence. Mary-Lynnette was trying very hard not to see things from Ash's point of view. At last she said, "So what do you want me to do?"

"Oh, I don't know, why don't we all have a pizza party and watch TV?" Ash sounded savage. "I have no idea what to do," he added in more normal tones. "And you'd better believe I've been thinking about it. The only thing I can come up with is that the girls have to go back with me, and we all have to lie through our teeth to Quinn."

Mary-Lynnette tried to think, but her head was throbbing.

"There is one other possibility," Ash said. He said it under his breath, as if he wouldn't mind if she pretended not to hear him.

Mary-Lynnette eased a crick in her neck, watching blue-and-yellow images of the sun on her shut eyelids. "What?"

"I know you and the girls did a blood-tie ceremony. It was illegal, but that's beside the point. *You're* part of the reason they don't want to leave here."

Mary-Lynnette opened her mouth to point out that they didn't want to leave because life had been unbearable for them in the Night World, but Ash hurried on. "But maybe if you were—like us, we could work something out. I could take the girls back to the island, and then in a few months I could get them out again. We'd go someplace where nobody would know us. Nobody would suspect there was anything irregular about you. The girls would be free, and you'd be there, so there's no reason they shouldn't be happy. Your brother could come, too."

Mary-Lynnette turned around slowly. She examined Ash. The sun brought out hidden warm tones in his hair, making it a shimmering blond somewhere between Jade's and Kestrel's. His eyes were shadowed, some dark color. He stood lanky and elegant as ever, but with one hand in his pocket and a pained expression on his face.

"Don't frown; you'll spoil your looks," she said.

"For God's sake, don't patronize me!" he yelled.

Mary-Lynnette was startled. Well. Okay.

"I *think*," she said, more cautiously but with emphasis to let him know that she was the one with a right to be upset, "that you are suggesting changing me into a vampire."

The corner of Ash's mouth jerked. He put his other hand in his pocket and looked away. "That was the general idea, yes."

"So that your sisters can be happy."

"So that you don't get killed by some vigilante like Quinn."

"But aren't the Night People going to kill me just the same if you change me?"

"Only if they *find* you," Ash said savagely. "And if we can get away from here clean, they wouldn't. Anyway, as a vampire you'd have a better chance of fighting them."

"So I'm supposed to become a vampire and leave everything I love here so your sisters can be happy."

Ash just stared angrily at the roof of the building across the street. "Forget it."

"Believe me, I wasn't even thinking about it in the first place."

"Fine." He continued to stare. All at once Mary-Lynnette had the horrible feeling that his eyes were wet.

And I've cried I don't know how many times in the last two days—and I only used to cry when the stars were so beautiful it hurt. There's something *wrong* with me now. I don't even know who I am anymore.

There seemed to be something wrong with Ash, too.

"Ash . . ."

He didn't look at her. His jaw was tight.

The problem is that there isn't any tidy answer, Mary-Lynnette thought. "I'm sorry," she said huskily, trying to shake off the strange feelings that had suddenly descended on her. "It's just that everything's turned out so . . . *weird.* I never asked for any of this." She swallowed. "I guess you never asked for it, either. First your sisters running away . . . and then me. Some joke, yeah?"

"Yeah." He wasn't staring off into the distance anymore. "Look . . . I might as well tell you. I *didn't* ask for this, and if somebody had said last week that I'd be in . . . involved . . . with a human, I'd have knocked his head off. I mean, after howls of derisive laughter. But."

He stopped. That seemed to be the end of his confession: *but.* Of course, he didn't really need to say more. Mary-Lynnette, arms folded over her chest, stared at a curved piece of glass on the ground and tried to think of other phrases that started with *in.* Besides the obvious. She couldn't come up with any.

She resisted the impulse to nudge the glass with her foot. "I'm a bad influence on your sisters."

"I said that to protect you. To try and protect you."

"I can protect myself."

"So I've noticed," he said dryly. "Does that help?"

"You noticing? No, because you don't really believe it. You'll always think I'm weaker than you, softer . . . even if you didn't *say* it, I'd know you were thinking it."

Ash suddenly looked crafty. His eyes were as green as

hellebore flowers. "If you were a vampire, you wouldn't *be* weaker," he said. "Also, you'd know what I was really thinking." He held out his hand. "Want a sample?"

Mary-Lynnette said abruptly, "We'd better get back. They're going to think we've killed each other."

"Let them," Ash said, his hand still held out, but Mary-Lynnette just shook her head and walked away.

She was scared. Wherever she'd been going with Ash, she'd been getting in too deep. And she wondered how much of their conversation had been audible around front.

When she rounded the corner, her eyes immediately went to Jeremy. He was standing with Kestrel by the gas pump. They were close together, and for just an instant Mary-Lynnette felt something like startled dismay.

Then her inner voice asked, Are you *insane*? You can't be jealous over him while you're worrying whether he's jealous over *you*, and meanwhile worrying about what to do with your soulmate. . . . It's *good* if he and Kestrel like each other.

"I don't care; I can't wait anymore," Jade was saying to Rowan on the sidewalk. "I've got to find him."

"She thinks Tiggy's gone home," Rowan said, seeing Mary-Lynnette. Ash went toward Rowan. Kestrel did, too. Somehow Mary-Lynnette was left beside Jeremy.

Once again, she didn't know the etiquette. She glanced at him—and stopped feeling awkward. He was watching her in his quiet, level way.

But then he startled her. He threw a look at the sidewalk and said, "Mary-Lynnette, be careful."

"What?"

"Be *careful.*" It was the same tone he'd used when warning her about Todd and Vic. Mary-Lynnette followed his gaze . . . to Ash.

"It's all right," Mary-Lynnette said. She didn't know how to explain. Even his own sisters hadn't believed Ash wouldn't hurt her.

Jeremy looked bleak. "I know guys like that. Sometimes they bring human girls to their clubs—and you don't want to know why. So just—just watch yourself, all right?"

It was a nasty shock. Rowan and the girls had said similar things, but coming from Jeremy it sank in, somehow. Ash had undoubtedly done things in his life that . . . well, that would make her want to kill him if she knew. Things you couldn't just forget about.

"I'll be careful," she said. She realized her fists were clenched, and she said with a glimmer of humor, "I can handle him."

Jeremy still looked bleak. His brown eyes were dark and his jaw was tight as he looked at Ash. Under his quietness, Mary-Lynnette could sense leashed power. Cold anger. Protectiveness. And the fact that he didn't like Ash *at all.*

The others were coming back. "I'll be all right," Mary-Lynnette whispered quickly.

Aloud, Jeremy said, "I'll keep thinking about the people around town. I'll tell you if I come up with something."

Mary-Lynnette nodded. "Thanks, Jeremy." She tried to give him a reassuring look as everybody got into the car.

He stood watching as she pulled out of the gas station. He didn't wave.

"Okay, so we go home," Mark said. "And then what?"

Nobody answered. Mary-Lynnette realized that she had no idea what.

"I guess we'd better figure out if we still have any suspects," she said at last.

"There's something else we've got to do, first," Rowan said softly. "We vampires, I mean."

Mary-Lynnette could tell just by the way she said it. But Mark asked, "What?"

"We need to feed," Kestrel said with her most radiant smile.

They got back to Burdock Farm. There was no sign of the cat. The four vampires headed for the woods, Jade calling for Tiggy, and Mary-Lynnette headed for Mrs. B.'s rolltop desk. She got engraved stationery—only slightly mildewed at the edges—and a silver pen with a fussy Victorian pattern on it. "Now," she said to Mark as she sat at the kitchen table. "We're going to play List the Suspects."

"There's nothing in this house to eat you know," Mark said. He had all the cupboards open. "Just things like instant coffee and green Jujyfruits. The ones everybody leaves."

"What can I say, your girlfriend is undead. Come on. Sit down and concentrate." Mark sat down and sighed. "Who have we got?"

"We should have gone to find out what the deal was with that horse," Mark said.

Mary-Lynnette stopped with her pen poised over the stationery. "You're right, that must be connected. I forgot about it." Which just goes to show you, detective work doesn't mix with l—with idle dawdling.

"All right," she said grimly. "So let's assume that whoever killed the horse was the same person who killed Aunt Opal and the goat. And maybe the same person who broke the gas station window—that happened last night, too. Where does that get us?"

"I think it was Todd and Vic," Mark said.

"You're not being helpful."

"I'm serious. You know how Todd is always chewing on that toothpick. And there were toothpicks stuck in the goat."

Toothpicks . . . now, what did *that* remind her of? No, not toothpicks, the bigger stakes. Why couldn't she *remember*?

She rubbed her forehead, giving up. "Okay . . . I'll put Todd and Vic, vampire hunters, with a question mark. Unless you think they're vampires themselves."

"Nope," Mark said, undeterred by her sarcasm. "I think Jade would've noticed *that* when she drank their blood." He eyed her thoughtfully. "You're the smart one. Who do *you* think did it?"

"I have no idea." Mark made a face at her, and she doodled a stake on the stationery. The doodle changed into a very small stake, more like a pencil, held by a feminine hand. She never could draw hands. . . .

"Oh, my God. *Bunny.*"

"Bunny did it?" Mark asked ingenuously, prepared to be straight man for a joke.

But Mary-Lynnette said, "*Yes.* I mean—no, I don't know. But those stakes in the goat—the big ones—I've seen her *using* them. She uses them on her nails. They're cuticle sticks."

"Well . . ." Mark looked dismayed. "But I mean . . . *Bunny.* C'mon. She can't kill a mosquito."

Mary-Lynnette shook her head, agitated. "Rowan said she had a lamia name. And she said something strange to me—Bunny—the day I was looking for Todd and Vic." It was all coming back now, a flood of memories that she didn't particularly want. "She said, 'Good hunting.'"

"Mare, it's from *The Jungle Book.*"

"I know. It was still weird for her to say. And she's almost *too* sweet and scared—what if it's all an act?" When Mark didn't answer, she said, "Is it any more unlikely than Todd and Vic being vampire hunters?"

"So put her down, too."

Mary-Lynnette did. Then she said, "You know, there's

something I keep meaning to ask Rowan—about how they wrote to Mrs. B. from that island—" She broke off and tensed as the back door banged.

"Am I the first one back?"

It was Rowan, windblown and glowing, slightly breathless. Her hair was a tumbling chestnut cloud around her.

"Where's everybody else?" Mary-Lynnette asked.

"We separated early on. It's the only way, you know, with four of us in this small of an area."

"Small!" Mark looked offended. "If Briar Creek has one good thing—and I'm not saying it does—it's space."

Rowan smiled. "For a hunting range, it *is* small," she said. "No offense. It's fine for us—we never got to hunt at all on the island. They brought our meals to us, tranquilized and completely passive."

Mary-Lynnette pushed away the image this evoked. "Um, you want to register a guess on Whodunit?"

Rowan sat down in a kitchen chair, smoothing a wisp of brown hair off her forehead. "I don't know. I wonder if it's somebody we haven't even thought of yet."

Mary-Lynnette remembered what she'd been talking about when the door banged. "Rowan, I always meant to ask you—you said that only Ash could have figured out where you were going when you ran away. But what about the guy who helped you smuggle letters off the island? *He* would know where your aunt lived, right? He could see the address on the letters."

"Crane Linden." Rowan smiled, a sad little smile. "No, he wouldn't know. He's . . ." She touched her temple lightly. "I don't know what you call it. His mind never developed completely. He can't read. But he's very kind."

There were illiterate vampires? Well, why not? Aloud Mary-Lynnette said, "Oh. Well, I guess it's one more person we can eliminate."

"Look, can we just brainstorm a minute?" Mark said. "This is probably crazy, but what if Jeremy's uncle isn't really dead? And what if—"

At that moment, there was a crash from the *front* porch.

No, a *tap-tap-crash,* Mary-Lynnette thought. Then she thought, Oh, God . . . *Tiggy.*

CHAPTER 15

T*iggy*.

She was running. Throwing the door open. Visions of kittens impaled by tiny stakes in her mind.

It wasn't Tiggy on the front porch. It was Ash. He was lying flat in the purple twilight, little moths fluttering around him.

Mary-Lynnette felt a violent wrench in her chest. For a moment everything seemed suspended—and changed.

If Ash were dead—if Ash had been killed . . .

Things would never be all right. *She* would never be all right. It would be like the night with the moon and stars gone. Nothing that anybody could do would make up for it. Mary-Lynnette didn't know why—it didn't make any sense—but she suddenly knew it was true.

She couldn't breathe and her arms and legs felt strange. Floaty. Out of her control.

Then Ash moved. He lifted his head and pushed up with his arms and looked around.

Mary-Lynnette could breathe again, but she still felt dizzy. "Are you hurt?" she asked stupidly. She didn't dare touch him. In her present state one blast of electricity could fry her circuits forever. She'd melt like the Wicked Witch of the West.

"I fell in this *hole*," he said. "What do you think?"

That's right, Mary-Lynnette thought; the footsteps *had* ended with more of a crash than a thud. Not like the footsteps of last night.

And that meant something . . . if only she could follow the thought to the end. . . .

"Having problems, Ash?" Kestrel's voice said sweetly, and then Kestrel herself appeared out of the shadows, looking like an angel with her golden hair and her lovely clean features. Jade was behind her, holding Tiggy in her arms.

"He was up in a tree," Jade said, kissing the kitten's head. "I had to talk him down." Her eyes were emerald in the porch light, and she seemed to float rather than walk.

Ash was getting up, shaking himself. Like his sisters, he looked uncannily beautiful after a feeding, with a sort of weird moonlight glow in his eyes. Mary-Lynnette's thought was long gone.

"Come on in," she said resignedly. "And help figure out who killed your aunt."

Now that Ash was indisputably all right, she wanted to forget what she'd been feeling a minute ago. Or at least not to think about what it meant.

What it means, the little voice inside her head said sweetly, is that you're in *big* trouble, girl. Ha ha.

"So what's the story?" Kestrel said briskly as they all sat around the kitchen table.

"The story is that there is no story," Mary-Lynnette said. She stared at her paper in frustration. "Look—what if we start at the beginning? We don't know who did it, but we do know some things about them. Right?"

Rowan nodded encouragingly. "Right."

"First: the goat. Whoever killed the goat had to be strong, because poking those toothpicks through hide wouldn't have been easy. And whoever killed the goat had to know how your uncle Hodge was killed, because the goat was killed in the same way. And they had to have some reason for putting a black iris in the goat's mouth—either because they knew Ash belonged to the Black Iris Club, or because they belonged to the Black Iris Club themselves."

"Or because they thought a black iris would represent all lamia, or all Night People," Ash said. His voice was muffled—he was bent over, rubbing his ankle. "That's a common mistake Outsiders make."

Very good, Mary-Lynnette thought in spite of herself. She said, "Okay. And they had access to two different kinds of small stakes—which isn't saying much, because you can buy both kinds in town."

"And they must have had some reason to hate Mrs. B., or to hate vampires," Mark said. "Otherwise, why kill her?"

Mary-Lynnette gave him a patient look. "I hadn't gotten to Mrs. B. yet. But we can do her now. First, whoever killed Mrs. B. obviously knew she was a vampire, because they staked her. And, second . . . um . . . second . . ." Her voice trailed off. She couldn't think of anything to go second.

"Second, they probably killed her on impulse," Ash said, in a surprisingly calm and analytical voice. "You said she was stabbed with a picket from the fence, and if they'd been planning on doing it, they'd probably have brought their own stake."

"*Very* good." This time Mary-Lynnette said it out loud. She couldn't help it. She met Ash's eyes and saw something that startled her. He looked as if it mattered to him that she thought he was smart.

Well, she thought. Well, well. Here we are, probably for the first time, just talking to each other. Not arguing, not being sarcastic, just talking. It's nice.

It was *surprisingly* nice. And the strange thing was, she knew Ash thought so, too. They understood each other. Over the table, Ash gave her a barely perceptible nod.

They kept talking. Mary-Lynnette lost track of time as they sat and argued and brainstormed. Finally she looked up at the clock and realized with a shock that it was near midnight.

"Do we *have* to keep thinking?" Mark said pathetically. "I'm tired." He was almost lying on the table. So was Jade.

I know how you feel, Mary-Lynnette thought. My brain is stalled. I feel . . . extremely stupid.

"Somehow, I don't think we're going to solve the murder tonight," Kestrel said. Her eyes were closed.

She was right. The problem was that Mary-Lynnette didn't feel like going to bed, either. She didn't want to lie down and relax—there was a restlessness inside her.

I want . . . what do I want? she thought. I want . . .

"If there weren't a psychopathic goat killer lurking around here, I'd go out and look at the stars," she said.

Ash said, as if it were the most natural thing in the world, "I'll go with you."

Kestrel and Jade looked at their brother in disbelief. Rowan bent her head, not quite hiding a smile.

Mary-Lynnette said, "Um . . ."

"Look," Ash said. "I don't think the goat killer is lurking out there every *minute* looking for people to skewer. And if anything does happen, I can handle it." He stopped, looked guilty, then bland. "I mean—*we* can handle it, because there'll be two of us."

Close but no cigar, buddy, Mary-Lynnette thought. Still, there was a certain basic truth to what he was saying. He was strong and fast, and she had the feeling he knew how to fight dirty.

Even if she'd never seen him do it, she thought suddenly. All those times she'd gone after him, shining light in his eyes, kicking him in the shins—and he'd never once tried to retaliate. She didn't think it had even occurred to him.

She looked at him and said, "Okay."

"Now," Mark said. "Look . . ."

"We'll be fine," Mary-Lynnette told him. "We won't go far."

Mary-Lynnette drove. She didn't know exactly where she was going, only that she didn't want to go to her hill. Too many weird memories. Despite what she'd told Mark, she found herself taking the car farther and farther. Out to where Hazel Green Creek and Beavercreek almost came together and the land between them was a good imitation of a rain forest.

"Is this the best place to look at stars?" Ash said doubtfully when they got out of the station wagon.

"Well—if you're looking straight up," Mary-Lynnette said. She faced eastward and tilted her head far back.

"See the brightest star up there? That's Vega, the queen star of summer."

"Yeah. She's been higher in the sky every night this summer," Ash said without emphasis.

Mary-Lynnette glanced at him.

He shrugged. "When you're out so much at night, you get

to recognize the stars," he said. "Even if you don't know their names."

Mary-Lynnette looked back up at Vega. She swallowed. "Can you—can you see something small and bright below her—something ring-shaped?"

"The thing that looks like a ghost doughnut?"

Mary-Lynnette smiled, but only with her lips. "That's the Ring Nebula. I can see that—with my telescope."

She could feel him looking at her, and she heard him take a breath as if he were going to say something. But then he let the breath out again and looked back up at the stars.

It was the perfect moment for him to mention something about how Vampires See It Better. And if he had, Mary-Lynnette would have turned on him and rejected him with righteous anger.

But since he *didn't*, she felt a different kind of anger welling up. A spring of contrariness, as if she were the Mary in the nursery rhyme. What, so you've decided I'm not good enough to be a vampire or something?

And what did I really bring you out here for, to the most isolated place I could find? Only for starwatching? I don't *think* so.

I don't even know who I am anymore, she remembered with a sort of fatalistic gloom. I have the feeling I'm about to surprise myself.

"Aren't you getting a crick in your neck?" Ash said.

Mary-Lynnette rolled her head from side to side slightly to limber the muscles. "Maybe."

"I could rub it for you?" He made the offer from several feet away.

Mary-Lynnette snorted and gave him a look.

The moon, a waning crescent, was rising above the cedars to the east. Mary-Lynnette said, "You want to take a walk?"

"Huh? Sure."

They walked and Mary-Lynnette thought. About how it would be to see the Ring Nebula with her own eyes, or the Veil Nebula without a filter. She could feel a longing for them so strong it was like a cable attached to her chest, pulling her upward.

Of course, *that* was nothing new. She'd felt it lots of times before, and usually she'd ended up buying another book on astronomy, another lens for her telescope. Anything to bring her closer to what she wanted.

But now I have a whole new temptation. Something bigger and scarier than I ever imagined.

What if I could be—more than I am now? The same person, but with sharper senses? A Mary-Lynnette who could *really* belong to the night?

She'd already discovered she wasn't exactly who she'd always thought. She was more violent—she'd kicked Ash, hadn't she? Repeatedly. And she'd admired the purity of

Kestrel's fierceness. She'd seen the logic in the kill-or-be-killed philosophy. She'd dreamed about the joy of hunting.

What else did it take to be a Night Person?

"There's something I've been wanting to say to you," Ash said.

"Hm." Do I want to encourage him or not?

But what Ash said was "Can we stop fighting now?"

Mary-Lynnette thought and then said seriously, "I don't know."

They kept walking. The cedars towered around them like pillars in a giant ruined temple. A dark temple. And underneath, the stillness was so enormous that Mary-Lynnette felt as if she were walking on the moon.

She bent and picked a ghostly wildflower that was growing out of the moss. Death camas. Ash bent and picked up a broken-off yew branch lying at the foot of a twisted tree. They didn't look at each other. They walked, with a few feet of space between them.

"You know, somebody told me this would happen," Ash said, as if carrying on some entirely different conversation they'd been having.

"That you'd come to a hick town and chase a goat killer?"

"That someday I'd care for someone—and it would hurt."

Mary-Lynnette kept on walking. She didn't slow or speed up. It was only her heart that was suddenly beating hard—in a mixture of dismay and exhilaration.

Oh, God—whatever was going to happen was happening.

"You're not like anybody I've ever met," Ash said.

"Well, *that* feeling is mutual."

Ash stripped some of the papery purple bark off his yew stick. "And, you see, it's difficult because what I've always thought about humans—what I was always raised to think . . ."

"I know what you've always thought," Mary-Lynnette said sharply. Thinking, *vermin.*

"But," Ash continued doggedly, "the thing is—and I know this is going to sound strange—that I seem to love you sort of desperately." He pulled more bark off his stick.

Mary-Lynnette didn't look at him. She couldn't speak.

"I've done everything I could to get rid of the feeling, but it just won't *go.* At first I thought if I left Briar Creek, I'd forget it. But now I know that was insane. Wherever I go, it's going *with* me. I can't kill it off. So I have to think of something else."

Mary-Lynnette suddenly felt *extremely* contrary. "Sorry," she said coldly. "But I'm afraid it's not very flattering to have somebody tell you that they love you against their will, against their reason, and even—"

"Against their character," Ash finished for her, bleakly. "Yeah, I know."

Mary-Lynnette stopped walking. She stared at him. "You have *not* read *Pride and Prejudice,*" she said flatly.

"Why not?"

"Because Jane Austen was a human."

He looked at her inscrutably and said, "How do you know?"

Good point. *Scary* point. How could she really know *who* in human history had been human? What about Galileo? Newton? Tycho Brahe?

"Well Jane Austen was a *woman*," she said, retreating to safer ground. "And you're a chauvinist pig."

"Yes, well, that I can't argue."

Mary-Lynnette started walking again. He followed.

"So now can I tell you how, um, ardently I love and admire you?"

Another quote. "I thought your sisters said you *partied* all the time."

Ash understood. "I do," he said defensively. "But the morning after partying you have to stay in bed. And if you're in bed you might as well read something."

They walked.

"After all, we *are* soulmates," Ash said. "I can't be *completely* stupid or I'd be completely wrong for you."

Mary-Lynnette thought about that. And about the fact that Ash sounded almost—humble. Which he had certainly never sounded before.

She said, "Ash . . . I don't know. I mean—we *are* wrong for each other. We're just basically incompatible. Even if I were a *vampire*, we'd be basically incompatible."

"Well." Ash whacked at something with his yew branch. He spoke as if he half expected to be ignored. "Well, about that . . . I think I could *possibly* change your mind."

"About what?"

"Being incompatible. I think we could be sort of fairly compatible if . . ."

"If?" Mary-Lynnette said as the silence dragged on.

"Well, if you could bring yourself to kiss me."

"*Kiss* you?"

"Yeah, I know it's a radical concept. I was pretty sure you wouldn't go for it." He whacked at another tree. "Of course humans *have* been doing it for thousands of years."

Watching him sideways, Mary-Lynnette said, "Would you kiss a three-hundred-pound gorilla?"

He blinked twice. "Oh, thank you."

"I didn't mean you looked like one."

"Don't tell me, let me guess. I smell like one?"

Mary-Lynnette bit her lip on a grim smile. "I mean you're that much stronger than I am. Would you kiss a female gorilla that could crush you with one squeeze? When you couldn't do anything about it?"

He glanced at *her* sideways. "Well, you're not *exactly* in that position, are you?"

Mary-Lynnette said, "Aren't I? It looks to me as if I'd have to become a vampire just to deal with you on an equal level."

Ash said, "Here."

He was offering her the yew branch. Mary-Lynnette stared at him.

"You want to give me your stick."

"It's not a stick, it's the way to deal with me on an equal level." He put one end of the branch against the base of his throat, and Mary-Lynnette saw that it was *sharp.* She reached out to take the other end and found the stick was surprisingly hard and heavy.

Ash was looking straight at her. It was too dark to see what color his eyes were, but his expression was unexpectedly sober.

"One good push would do it," he said. "First here and then in the heart. You could eliminate the problem of me from your life."

Mary-Lynnette pushed, but gently. He took a step back. And another. She backed him up against a tree, holding the stick to his neck like a sword.

"I actually meant only if you were really serious," Ash said as he came up short against the cedar's bare trunk. But he didn't make a move to defend himself. "And the truth is that you don't even need a spear like that. A pencil in the right place would do it."

Mary-Lynnette narrowed her eyes at him, swirling the yew stick over his body like a fencer getting the range.

Then she removed it. She dropped it to the ground.

"You really have changed," she said.

Ash said simply, "I've changed so much in the last few days that I don't even recognize myself in the mirror."

"And you didn't kill your aunt."

"You're just now figuring that out?"

"No. But I always wondered just a bit. All right, I'll kiss you."

It was a little awkward, lining up to get the position right. Mary-Lynnette had never kissed a boy before. But once she started she found it was simple.

And . . . *now* she saw what the electric feeling of being soulmates was for. All the sensations she'd felt when touching his hand, only intensified. And not unpleasant. It was only unpleasant if you were afraid of it.

Afterward, Ash pulled away. "There. You see," he said shakily.

Mary-Lynnette took a few deep breaths. "I suppose that's what it feels like to fall into a black hole."

"Oh. Sorry."

"No, I mean—it was interesting." Singular, she thought. Different from anything she'd ever felt before. And she had the feeling that *she* would be different from now on, that she could never go back and be the same person she had been.

So who am I now? Somebody fierce, I think. Somebody who'd enjoy running through the darkness, underneath stars bright as miniature suns, and maybe even hunt deer. Somebody who can laugh at death the way the sisters do.

I'll discover a supernova and I'll hiss when somebody threatens me. I'll be beautiful and scary and dangerous and of course I'll kiss Ash a lot.

She was giddy, almost soaring with exhilaration.

I've always loved the night, she thought. And I'll finally belong to it completely.

"Mary-Lynnette?" Ash said hesitantly. "Did you *like* it?"

She blinked and looked at him. Focused.

"I want you to turn me into a vampire," she said.

It didn't feel like a jellyfish sting this time. It was quick and almost pleasant—like pressure being released. And then Ash's lips were on her neck, and that was *definitely* pleasant. Warmth radiated from his mouth. Mary-Lynnette found herself stroking the back of his neck and realized that his hair was soft, as nice to touch as cat's fur.

And his mind . . . was every color of the spectrum. Crimson and gold, jade and emerald and deep violet-blue. A tangled thorn-forest of iridescent colors that changed from second to second. Mary-Lynnette was dazzled.

And half frightened. There was darkness in among those gemlike colors. Things Ash had done in the past . . . things she could sense he was ashamed of now. But shame didn't change the acts themselves.

I know it doesn't—but I'll make up for them, somehow. You'll see; I'll find a way. . . .

So that's telepathy, Mary-Lynnette thought. She could *feel* Ash as he said the words, feel that he meant them with desperate earnestness—and feel that there was a lot to make up for.

I don't care. I'm going to be a creature of darkness, too. I'll do what's in my nature, with no regrets.

When Ash started to lift his head, she tightened her grip, trying to keep him there.

"Please don't tempt me," Ash said out loud, his voice husky, his breath warm on her neck. "If I take too much, it will make you seriously weak. I *mean* it, sweetheart."

She let him go. He picked up the yew stick and made a small cut at the base of his throat, tilting his head back like a guy shaving his chin.

"Ow."

Mary-Lynnette realized he'd never done this before. With a feeling that was almost awe, she put her lips to his neck.

I'm drinking blood. I'm a hunter already—sort of. Anyway, I'm drinking blood and liking it—maybe because it doesn't *taste* like blood. Not like copper and fear. It tastes weird and magic and old as the stars.

When Ash gently detached her, she swayed on her feet.

"We'd better go home," he said.

"Why? I'm okay."

"You're going to get dizzier—and weaker. And if we're going to finish changing you into a vampire—"

"If?"

"All right, *when*. But before we do, we need to talk. I need to explain it all to you; we have to figure out the details. And *you* need to rest."

Mary-Lynnette knew he was right. She wanted to stay here, alone with Ash in the dark cathedral of the forest—but she *did* feel weak. Languid. Apparently it was hard work becoming a creature of darkness.

They headed back the way they had come. Mary-Lynnette could feel the change inside herself—it was stronger than when she'd exchanged blood with the three girls. She felt simultaneously weak and hypersensitive. As if every pore were open.

The moonlight seemed much brighter. She could see colors clearly—the pale green of drooping cedar boughs, the eerie purple of parrot-beak wildflowers growing out of the moss.

And the forest wasn't silent anymore. She could hear faint uncanny sounds like the soft seething of needles in the wind, and her own footsteps on moist and fungus-ridden twigs.

I can even smell better, she thought. This place smells like incense cedar, and decomposing plants, and something really wild—feral, like something from the zoo. And something hot . . . burny . . .

Mechanical. It stung her nostrils. She stopped and looked at Ash in alarm.

"What *is* that?"

He'd stopped, too. "Smells like rubber and oil. . . ."

"Oh, God, the *car*," Mary-Lynnette said. They looked at each other for a moment, then simultaneously turned, breaking into a run.

It was the car. White smoke billowed from under the closed hood. Mary-Lynnette started to go closer, but Ash pulled her back to the side of the road.

"I just want to open the hood—"

"No. Look. There."

Mary-Lynnette looked—and gasped. Tiny tongues of flame were darting underneath the smoke. Licking out of the engine.

"Claudine always said this would happen," she said grimly as Ash pulled her back farther. "Only I think she meant it would happen with me in it."

"We're going to have to walk home," Ash said. "Unless maybe somebody sees the fire. . . ."

"Not a chance," Mary-Lynnette said. And *that's* what you get for taking a boy out to the most isolated place in Oregon, her inner voice said triumphantly.

"I don't suppose you could turn into a bat or something and fly back," she suggested.

"Sorry, I flunked shapeshifting. And I wouldn't leave you here alone anyway."

Mary-Lynnette still felt reckless and dangerous—and it made her impatient.

"I can take care of myself," she said.

And *that* was when the club came down and Ash pitched forward unconscious.

CHAPTER 16

After that, things happened very fast, and at the same time with a dreamy slowness. Mary-Lynnette felt her arms grabbed from behind. Something was pulling her hands together—something *strong.* Then she felt the bite of cord on her wrists, and she realized what was happening.

Tied up—I'm going to be helpless—I've got to *do* something fast. . . .

She fought, trying to wrench herself away, trying to kick. But it was already too late. Her hands were secure behind her back—and some part of her mind noted distantly that no wonder people on cop shows yell when they're handcuffed. It *hurt.* Her shoulders gave a shriek of agony as she was dragged backward up against a tree.

"Stop fighting," a voice snarled. A thick, distorted voice she didn't recognize. She tried to see who it was, but the tree was in the way. "If you relax it won't hurt."

Mary-Lynnette kept fighting, but it didn't make any difference. She could feel the deeply furrowed bark of the tree against her hands and back—and now she couldn't move.

Oh, God, oh, God—I can't get *away*. I was already weak from what Ash and I did—and now I can't move at all.

Then stop panicking and *think*, her inner voice said fiercely. Use your *brain* instead of getting hysterical.

Mary-Lynnette stopped struggling. She stood panting and tried to get control of her terror.

"I told you. It only hurts when you fight. A lot of things are like that," the voice said.

Mary-Lynnette twisted her head and saw who it was.

Her heart gave a sick lurch. She shouldn't have been surprised, but she was—surprised and infinitely disappointed.

"Oh, Jeremy," she whispered.

Except that it was a different Jeremy than the one she knew. His face was the same, his hair, his clothes—but there was something weird about him, something powerful and scary and . . . *unknowable.* His eyes were as inhuman and flat as a shark's.

"I don't want to hurt you," he said in that distorted stranger's voice. "I only tied you up because I didn't want you to interfere."

Mary-Lynnette's mind was registering different things in different layers. One part said, *My God, he's trying to be friendly,* and another part said, *To interfere with what?,* and a third part just kept saying *Ash.*

She looked at Ash. He was lying very still, and Mary-Lynnette's wonderful new eyes that could see colors in moonlight saw that his blond hair was slowly soaking with blood. On the ground beside him was a club made of yew—made of the hard yellow sapwood. No wonder he was unconscious.

But if he's bleeding he's not dead—oh, God, please, he *can't* be dead—Rowan said that only staking and burning kill vampires. . . .

"I have to take care of him," Jeremy said. "And then I'll let you go, I promise. Once I explain everything, you'll understand."

Mary-Lynnette looked up from Ash to the stranger with Jeremy's face. With a shock, she realized what he meant by "take care of." Three words that were just part of life to a hunter—to a werewolf.

So now I know about werewolves. They're killers—and I was right all along. I was right and Rowan was wrong.

"It'll only take a minute," Jeremy said—and his lips drew back.

Mary-Lynnette's heart seemed to slam violently inside her chest. Because his lips went farther up than any human's lips could. She could see his gums, whitish-pink. And she could see why his voice didn't sound like Jeremy's—it was his *teeth.*

White teeth in the moonlight. The teeth from her dream. Vampire teeth were nothing compared to this. The incisors at the front were made for cutting flesh from prey, the canines were two inches long, the teeth behind them looked designed for slicing and shearing.

Mary-Lynnette suddenly remembered something Vic Kimble's father had said three years ago. He'd said that a wolf could snap off the tail of a full-grown cow clean as pruning shears. He'd been complaining that somebody had let a wolf-dog crossbreed loose and it was going after his cattle. . . .

Except that of course it wasn't a crossbreed, Mary-Lynnette thought. It was Jeremy. I saw him every day at school—and then he must have gone home to look like *this.* To hunt.

Just now, as he stood over Ash with his teeth all exposed and his chest heaving, Jeremy looked completely, quietly insane.

"But *why*?" Mary-Lynnette burst out. "*Why* do you want to hurt him?"

Jeremy looked up—and she got another shock. His eyes were different. Before she'd seen them flash white in the darkness. Now they had no whites at all. They were brown with large liquid pupils. The eyes of an animal.

So it doesn't need to be a full moon, she thought. He can change anytime.

"Don't you know?" he said. "Doesn't anybody *understand*? This is *my* territory."

Oh. *Oh* . . .

So it was as simple as that. After all their brainstorming and arguing and detective work. In the end it was something as basic as an animal protecting its range.

"For a hunting range, it is small," Rowan had said.

"They were taking *my* game," Jeremy said. "My deer, my squirrels. They didn't have any right to do that. I tried to make them leave—but they wouldn't. They stayed and they kept killing. . . ."

He stopped talking—but a new sound came from him. It started out almost below the range of Mary-Lynnette's hearing—but the deep rumbling of it struck some primal chord of terror in her. It was as uncanny and inhuman as the danger-hum of an attacking swarm of bees.

Growling. He was growling. And it was *real.* The snarling growl a dog makes that tells you to turn and run. The sound it makes before it springs at your throat. . . .

"Jeremy!" Mary-Lynnette screamed. She threw herself forward, ignoring the white blaze of pain in her shoulders. But the cord held. She was jerked back. And Jeremy fell on Ash, lunging down, head darting forward like a striking snake, like a biting dog, like every animal that kills with its teeth.

Mary-Lynnette heard someone screaming *"No!"* and only later realized that it was her. She was fighting with the cord, and she could feel stinging and wetness at her wrists. But she couldn't get free and she couldn't stop seeing what was happening in front of her. And all the time that eerie, vicious growling that reverberated in Mary-Lynnette's own head and chest.

That was when things went cold and clear. Some part of Mary-Lynnette that was stronger than the panic took over. It stepped back and looked at the entire scene by the roadside: the car, which was still burning, sending clouds of choking white smoke whenever the wind blew the right way; the limp figure of Ash on the pine needles; the blur of snarling motion that was Jeremy.

"Jeremy!" she said, and her throat hurt, but her voice was calm—and commanding. "Jeremy—before you do that—don't you want me to *understand*? You said that was what you wanted. Jeremy, *help me understand.*"

For a long second she thought in dismay that it wasn't going to work. That he couldn't even hear her. But then his head lifted. She saw his face; she saw the blood on his chin.

Don't scream, don't scream, Mary-Lynnette told herself frantically. Don't show any shock. You have to keep him talking, keep him away from Ash.

Behind her back her hands were working automatically, as if trying to get out of ropes was something they'd always known how to do. The slick wetness actually helped. She could feel the cords slide a little.

"Please help me understand," she said again, breathless, but trying to hold Jeremy's eyes. "I'm your friend—you know that. We go back a long way."

Jeremy's whitish gums were streaked with red. He still had human features, but there was nothing at all human about that face.

Now, though—slowly—his lips came down to cover his gums. He looked more like a person and less like an animal. And when he spoke, his voice was distorted, but she could recognize it as Jeremy's voice.

"We do go back," he said. "I've watched you since we were kids—and I've seen you watching me."

Mary-Lynnette nodded. She couldn't get any words out.

"I always figured that someday, when we were older—maybe we'd be together. I thought maybe I could make you understand. About me. About everything. I thought you were the one person who might not be afraid. . . ."

"I'm not," Mary-Lynnette said, and hoped her voice wasn't shaking too badly. She was saying it to a figure in a blood-spattered shirt crouching over a torn body like a beast still ready to attack. Mary-Lynnette didn't dare look at Ash to see how badly he was hurt. She kept her eyes locked on Jeremy's. "And I think I can understand. You killed Mrs. Burdock, didn't you? Because she was on your territory."

"Not *her*," Jeremy said, and his voice was sharp with impatience. "She was just an old lady—she didn't hunt. I didn't mind having her in my range. I even did things for her, like fixing her fence and porch for free. . . . And that's when she told me *they* were coming. Those girls."

Just the way she told me, Mary-Lynnette thought, with dazed revelation. And he was there fixing the fence—of course. The way he does odd jobs for everybody.

"I *told* her it wouldn't work." Mary-Lynnette could hear it again—the beginnings of a snarling growl. Jeremy was tense and trembling, and she could feel herself start to tremble, too. "Three more hunters in this little place . . . I *told* her, but she wouldn't listen. She couldn't see. So then I lost my temper."

Don't look at Ash, don't call attention to him, Mary-Lynnette thought desperately. Jeremy's lips were drawing back again as if he needed something to attack. At the same time the distant part of her mind said, *So that's why he used a picket—Ash was right; it was an impulse of the moment.*

"Well, anybody can lose their temper," she said, and even though her voice cracked and there were tears in her eyes, Jeremy seemed to calm a little.

"Afterward, I thought maybe it was for the best," he said, sounding tired. "I thought when the girls found her, they'd know they had to leave. I waited for them to do it. I'm good at waiting."

He was staring past her, into the woods. Heart pounding, Mary-Lynnette grabbed the opportunity to dart a look at Ash.

Oh, God, he's not moving at all. And there's so much *blood.* . . . I've never seen so much blood. . . .

She twisted her wrists back and forth, trying to find some give in the cords.

"I watched, but they didn't go away," Jeremy said. Mary-Lynnette's eyes jerked back to him. "Instead *you* came. I heard Mark talking to Jade in the garden. She said she'd decided she was going to like it here. And then . . . I got mad. I made a noise and they heard me."

His face was changing. The flesh was actually moving in front of Mary-Lynnette's eyes. His cheekbones were broadening, his nose and mouth jutting. Hair was creeping between his eyebrows, turning them into a straight bar. She could *see* individual coarse hairs sprouting, dark against pale skin.

I'm going to be sick. . . .

"What's wrong, Mary-Lynnette?" He got up and she saw that his body was changing, too. It was still a human body, but it was too thin—stretched out. As if it were just long bones and sinews.

"Nothing's wrong," Mary-Lynnette got out in a whisper. She twisted violently at her cords—and felt one hand slide.

That's it. Now keep him distracted, keep him moving away from Ash. . . .

"Go on," she said breathlessly. "What happened then?"

"I knew I had to send them a message. I came back the next night for the goat—but you were there again. You ran away from me into the shed." He moved closer again and the moonlight caught his eyes—and *reflected.* The pupils shone greenish-orange. Mary-Lynnette could only stare.

That shadow in the clearing—those eyes I saw. Not a coyote. *Him.* He was following us everywhere.

The very thought made her skin creep. But there was another thought that was worse—the picture of him killing the goat. Doing it carefully, methodically—as a message.

That was why he didn't eat the heart and liver, Mary-Lynnette realized. He didn't kill it for food—it wasn't a normal werewolf killing. And *he's* not a normal werewolf.

He wasn't at all like what Rowan had described—a noble animal that hunted to eat. Instead he was . . . a mad dog.

Of all people, *Ash* had it right. Him and his jokes about rabies . . .

"You're so beautiful, you know," Jeremy said suddenly. "I've always thought that. I love your hair."

He was right in her face. She could see the individual pores in his skin with coarse hairs growing out of them. And she could *smell* him—the feral smell of a zoo.

He reached out to touch her hair, and his hand had dark, thick fingernails. Mary-Lynnette could feel her eyes getting wider. Say something . . . say something . . . don't show you're afraid.

"You knew how Mrs. Burdock's husband was killed," she got out.

"She told me a long time ago," Jeremy said almost absently, still moving his fingers in her hair. He'd changed so much that his voice was getting hard to understand. "I used little sticks from my models . . . you know I make models. And a black iris for *him.* Ash." Jeremy said the name with pure hatred. "I saw him that day with his stupid T-shirt. The Black Iris Club . . . my uncle belonged to that once. They treated him like he was second-class."

His eyes were inches from Mary-Lynnette's; she felt the brush of a fingernail on her ear. Suddenly she had the strength to give a violent wrench behind her back—and one hand came free. She froze, afraid that Jeremy would notice.

"I threw the goat on the porch and ran," Jeremy said, almost crooning the words as he petted Mary-Lynnette. "I knew you were all in there. I was so mad—I killed that horse and I kept running. I smashed the gas station window. I was going to burn it down—but then I decided to wait."

Yes, and yes, and yes, Mary-Lynnette thought even as she carefully worked her other wrist free, even as she stared into Jeremy's crazy eyes and smelled his animal breath. Yes, of course it was you we heard running away—and you didn't fall into the hole in the porch because you knew it was there, because you were fixing it. And yes, you were the one who smashed the window—who else would hate the gas station but somebody who worked there?

Her fingers eased the cord off her other wrist. She felt a surge of fierce triumph—but she controlled her expression and clenched her hands, trying to think of what to do. He was so strong and so quick . . . if she just threw herself at him, she wouldn't have a chance.

"And today you all came to town together," Jeremy said,

finishing the story quietly, through a mouth so inhuman it was hard to believe it could speak English. "I heard the way *he* was talking to you. I knew he wanted you—and he wanted to change you into one of *them.* I had to protect you from that."

Mary-Lynnette said almost steadily, "I knew you wanted to protect me. I could tell, Jeremy." She was feeling over the furrowed hemlock bark behind her. How could she attack him when she didn't even have a stick for a weapon? And even if she *had*, wood was no good. He wasn't a vampire.

Jeremy stepped back. Relief washed over Mary-Lynnette—for one second. Then she saw with horror that he was plucking at his shirt, pulling it off. And underneath . . . there was no skin. Instead there was hair. A pelt that twitched and shivered in the night air. "I followed you here and I fixed your car so you couldn't leave," Jeremy said. "I heard you say you wanted to be a vampire."

"Jeremy—that was just talk. . . ."

He went on as if she hadn't spoken. "But that was a mistake. Werewolves are much better. You'll understand when I show you. The moon looks so beautiful when you're a wolf."

Oh, *God*—and so that was what he meant by protecting her, by making her understand. He meant changing her into something like him.

I need a weapon.

Rowan had said silver was harmful to werewolves, so the old silver-bullet legend must be true. But she didn't *have* a silver bullet. Or even a silver dagger . . .

A silver dagger . . . a silver *knife* . . .

Behind Jeremy the station wagon was almost invisible in the clouds of smoke. And by now the smoke had the red glow of uncontrolled fire.

It's too dangerous, Mary-Lynnette thought. It's about to go. I'd never make it in and out. . . .

Jeremy was still talking, his voice savage now. "You won't miss the Night World. All their stupid restrictions—no killing humans, no hunting too often. *Nobody* tells me how to hunt. My uncle tried, but I took care of him—"

Suddenly the creature—it wasn't really a person anymore—broke off and turned sharply. Mary-Lynnette saw its lips go back again, saw its teeth parted and ready to bite. In the same instant she saw why—Ash was moving.

Sitting up, even though his throat was cut. Looking around dazedly. He saw Mary-Lynnette, and his eyes seemed to focus. Then he looked at the thing Jeremy had become.

"You—get away from her!" he shouted in a voice Mary-Lynnette had never heard before. A voice filled with deadly fury. Mary-Lynnette could see him change position in a swift, graceful motion, gathering his muscles under him to jump—

But the werewolf jumped first. Springing like an animal—except that Jeremy still had arms, and one hand went for the yew club. The club smashed sideways into Ash's head and knocked him flat. And then it fell, bouncing away on the carpet of needles.

The werewolf didn't need it—it was baring its teeth. It was going to tear Ash's throat out, like the horse, like the hiker . . .

Mary-Lynnette was running.

Not toward Ash. She couldn't help him bare-handed. She ran toward the car, into the clouds of choking smoke.

Oh, God, it's hot. Please let me just get there. . . .

She could feel the heat on her cheeks, on her arms. She remembered something from an elementary school safety class and dropped to her knees, scrambling and crawling where the air was cooler.

And then she heard the sound behind her. The most eerie sound there is—a wolf howling.

It knows what I'm doing. It's seen that knife every time I pry off my gas cap. It's going to stop me. . . .

She threw herself blindly into the smoke and heat, and reached the car. Orange flames were shooting crazily from the engine, and the door handle burned her hand when she touched it. She fumbled, wrenching at it.

Open, *open* . . .

The door swung out. Hot air blasted around her. If she'd been completely human she wouldn't have been able to stand it. But she'd exchanged blood with four vampires in two days, and she wasn't completely human anymore. She wasn't Mary-Lynnette anymore . . . but was she capable of killing?

Flames were licking up beneath the dashboard. She groped over smoking vinyl and shoved a hand under the driver's seat.

Find it! Find it!

Her fingers touched metal—the knife. The silver fruit knife with the Victorian scrolling that she'd borrowed from Mrs. Burdock. It was very hot. Her hand closed on it, and she pulled it from under the seat and turned . . . just as something came flying at her from behind.

The turning was instinctive—she had to face what was attacking her. But what she would always know afterward was that she could have turned without pointing the *knife* at what was attacking her. There was a moment in which she could have slanted it backward or toward the ground or toward herself. And if she'd been the Mary-Lynnette of the old days, she might have done that.

She didn't. The knife faced outward. Toward the shape jumping at her. And when the thing landed on top of her she felt impact in her wrist and all the way up her arm.

The distant part of her mind said, It went in cleanly between the ribs. . . .

And then everything was very confused. Mary-Lynnette felt teeth in her hair, snapping for her neck. She felt claws scratching at her, leaving welts on her arms. The thing attacking her was hairy and heavy and it wasn't a person or even a half-person. It was a large, snarling wolf.

She was still holding the knife, but it was hard to keep her grip on it. It jerked around, twisting her wrist in an impossible direction. It was buried in the wolf's chest.

For just an instant, as the thing pulled away, she got a good look at it.

A beautiful animal. Sleek and handsome, but with crazy eyes. It was trying to kill her with its last panting breath.

Oh, God, you hate me, don't you? I've chosen Ash over you; I've hurt you with silver. And now you're dying. You must feel so betrayed. . . .

Mary-Lynnette began to shake violently. She couldn't do this anymore. She let go of the knife and pushed and kicked at the wolf with her arms and legs. Half scrambling and half scooting on her back, she managed to get a few feet away. The wolf stood silhouetted against a background of fire. She could see it gather itself for one last spring at her—

There was a very soft, contained *poof.* The entire car lurched like something in agony—and then the fireball was everywhere.

Mary-Lynnette cringed against the ground, half-blinded, but she had to watch.

So that's what it looks like. A car going up in flames. Not the kind of big explosion you hear in the movies. Just a *poof.* And then just the fire, going up and up.

The heat drove her away, still crawling, but she couldn't stop looking. Orange flames. That was all her station wagon was now. Orange flames shooting every which way out of a metal skeleton on tires.

The wolf didn't come out of the flames.

Mary-Lynnette sat up. Smoke was in her throat, and when she tried to yell "Jeremy!" it came out as a hoarse croak.

The wolf still didn't come out. And no wonder, with a silver knife in its chest and fire all around it.

Mary-Lynnette sat, arms wrapped around herself, and watched the car burn.

He would have killed me. Like any good hunter. I had to defend myself, I had to save Ash. And the girls . . . he would have killed all of them. And then he'd have killed more people like that hiker. . . . He was crazy and completely *evil*, because he'd do anything to get what he wanted.

And she'd seen it from the beginning. Something under that "nice guy" exterior—she'd seen it over and over, but she'd kept letting herself get convinced it wasn't there. She should have trusted her feelings in the first place. When she'd realized that she'd solved the mystery of Jeremy Lovett and that it wasn't a happy ending.

She was shaking but she couldn't cry.

The fire roared on. Tiny sparks showered upward.

I don't care if it was justified. It wasn't like killing in my dream. It wasn't easy and it wasn't natural and I'll never forget the way he looked at me. . . .

Then she thought, *Ash.*

She'd been so paralyzed she'd almost forgotten him. Now she turned around, almost too frightened to look. She made herself crawl over to where he was still lying.

So much blood . . . how can he be all right? But if he's dead . . . if it's all been for nothing . . .

But Ash was breathing. And when she touched his face, trying to find a clean place in the blood, he moved. He stirred, then he tried to sit up.

"Stay there." Jeremy's shirt and jeans were on the ground. Mary-Lynnette picked up the shirt and dabbed at Ash's neck. "Ash, keep still. . . ."

He tried to sit up again. "Don't worry. I'll protect you."

"Lie down," Mary-Lynnette said. When he didn't, she pushed at him. "There's nothing to do. He's dead."

He sank back, eyes shutting. "Did I kill him?"

Mary-Lynnette made a choked sound that wasn't exactly a laugh. She was trembling with relief—Ash could breathe and talk, and he even sounded like his normal fatuous self. She'd had no idea how good that could sound. And underneath the swabbing shirt she could see that his neck was already healing. What had been gashes were becoming flat pink scars.

Vampire flesh was incredible.

Ash swallowed. "You didn't answer my question."

"No. You didn't kill him. I did."

His eyes opened. They just looked at each other for a moment. And in that moment Mary-Lynnette knew they were both realizing a lot of things.

Then Ash said, "I'm sorry," and his voice had never been less fatuous. He pushed the shirt away and sat up. "I'm so sorry."

She didn't know who reached first, but they were holding each other. And Mary-Lynnette was thinking about hunters and danger and laughing at death. About all the things it meant to *really* belong to the night. And about how she would never look in the mirror and see the same person she used to see.

"At least it's over now," Ash said. She could feel his arms around her, his warmth and solidity, his support. "There won't be any more killings. It's over."

It was, and so were a lot of other things.

The first sob was hard to get out. So hard that she'd have thought there would be a pause before the next—but, no. There was no pause between that one and the next, or the next or the next. She cried for a long time. And the fire burned itself out and the sparks flew upward and Ash held her all the while.

CHAPTER 17

"Well, she wasn't telling humans anything—but she did defy the authority of the Night World," Ash said in his most lazy, careless voice.

Quinn said succinctly, "How?"

It was late Monday afternoon and the sun was streaming through the western windows of the Burdock farmhouse. Ash was wearing a brand-new shirt bought at the Briar Creek general store, a turtleneck with long sleeves that covered the almost-healed scars on his throat and arms. His jeans were bleached white, his hair was combed over the scab on the back of his head, and he was playing the scene of his life.

"She knew about a rogue werewolf and didn't tell anybody about him."

"So she was a traitor. And what did you do?"

Ash shrugged. "Staked her."

Quinn laughed out loud.

"No, really," Ash said earnestly, looking into Quinn's face with what he knew were wide, guileless eyes—probably blue. "See?"

Without taking his eyes from Quinn's he whipped a pink-and-green country quilt off the bundle on the couch.

Quinn's eyebrows flew upward.

He stared for a moment at Aunt Opal, who had been cleaned so that you'd never know she'd ever been buried, and who had the picket stake carefully replaced in her chest.

Quinn actually swallowed. It was the first time Ash had ever seen him falter.

"You really did it," he said. There was reluctant respect in his voice—and definite shock.

You know, Quinn, Ash thought, I don't think you're quite as tough as you pretend. After all, no matter how you try to act like an Elder, you're only eighteen. And you'll *always* be eighteen, and next year maybe I'll be older.

"Well," Quinn said, blinking rapidly. "Well. Well—I have to hand it to you."

"Yeah, I just decided the best thing to do was clean up the whole situation. She was getting on, you know."

Quinn's dark eyes widened fractionally. "I have to admit—I didn't think you were *that* ruthless."

"You've gotta do what you've gotta do. For the family honor, of course."

Quinn cleared his throat. "So—what about the werewolf?"

"Oh, I took care of that, too." Ash meandered over and

whipped a brown-and-white quilt off Exhibit B. The wolf was a charred and contorted corpse. It had given Mary-Lynnette hysterics when Ash insisted on pulling it out of the car, and Quinn's nostrils quivered when he looked at it.

"Sorry, it does smell like burnt hair, doesn't it? I got a little sooty myself, keeping him in the fire. . . ."

"You burned him *alive*?"

"Well, it is one of the traditional methods. . . ."

"Just put the blanket back, all right?"

Ash put the blanket back.

"So, you see, everything's taken care of. No humans involved, no extermination necessary."

"Yes, all right . . ." Quinn's eyes were still on the quilt. Ash decided the moment was right.

"And by the way, it turns out the girls had a perfectly legitimate reason for coming. They just wanted to learn to hunt. Nothing illegal about that, is there?"

"What? Oh. No." Quinn glanced at Aunt Opal, then finally looked back at Ash. "So they're coming back now that they've learned it."

"Well, eventually. They haven't quite learned it yet . . . so they're staying."

"They're *staying*?"

"Right. Look, I'm the head of the family on the West Coast, aren't I? And I say they're staying."

"Ash . . ."

"It's about time there was a Night World outpost in this area, don't you think? You see what's happened without one. You get families of outlaw werewolves wandering around. Somebody's got to stay here and hold down the fort."

"Ash . . . you couldn't *pay* Night People to strand themselves out here. Nothing but animals to feed on, nobody but humans to associate with . . ."

"Yeah, it's a dirty job, but someone's got to do it. Besides, wasn't it you who said it's not good living your whole life isolated on an island?"

Quinn stared at him, then said, "Well, I don't think this is much better."

"Then it serves my sisters right. Maybe in a few years they'll appreciate the island more. Then they can hand the job over to someone else."

"Ash . . . no one else is going to *come* here."

"Well." With the battle won, and Quinn simply looking dazed and as if he wanted to get back to Los Angeles as fast as possible, Ash allowed himself a small measure of truth.

"I might come visit them someday," he said.

"He did a beautiful job," Rowan said that evening. "We heard it all from the kitchen. You would have loved it."

Mary-Lynnette smiled.

"Quinn can't wait to get away," Jade said, intertwining her fingers with Mark's.

Kestrel said to Ash, "I'd just like to be around when you explain all this to Dad."

"That's funny," Ash said. "I feel just the opposite."

Everyone laughed—except Mary-Lynnette. The big farm kitchen was warm and bright, but the windows were darkening. She couldn't see anything in the gathering darkness—in the last two days the effects of her blood exchange had faded. Her senses were ordinary human senses again.

"You're sure you won't get in trouble?" she asked Ash.

"No. I'll tell our dad the truth—mostly. That an outlaw werewolf killed Aunt Opal and that I killed the werewolf. And that the girls are better off here, hunting quietly and watching out for other rogues. There's sure to be some record of the Lovett family. . . . Dad can check out the history all he wants."

"A whole family of outlaw werewolves," Kestrel said musingly.

"Of *crazy* werewolves," Ash said. "They were as dangerous to the Night World as any vampire hunters could be. God knows how long they've been here—long enough for their land to get named Mad Dog Creek."

"And for people to mistake them for Sasquatch," Mark said.

Rowan's brown eyes were troubled. "And it was my fault that you didn't know," she said to Mary-Lynnette. "*I* told you he couldn't be the killer. I'm sorry."

Mary-Lynnette captured her gaze and held it. "Rowan, you

are *not* going to feel guilty for this. You couldn't have realized. He wasn't killing for food like a normal werewolf. He was killing to protect his territory—and to scare us."

"And it might have worked," Mark said. "Except that you guys didn't have anywhere else to go."

Ash looked at Mark, then at his sisters. "I have a question. Is the territory around here going to be enough for *you*?"

"Of course," Rowan said, with gentle surprise.

"We don't always need to *kill* the animals," Jade said. "We're getting it down pat now. We can take a little here and a little there. Heck, we can even try the *goat*."

"I'd rather try Tiggy," Kestrel said, and for a moment her golden eyes glimmered. Mary-Lynnette didn't say it, but she wondered sometimes about Kestrel. If maybe, someday, Kestrel might need a bigger territory of her own. She was a lot like Jeremy in some ways.

Beautiful, ruthless, single-minded. A true Night Person.

"And what about you?" Ash said, looking at Mark.

"Me? Uh . . . Well, when you get down to it, I'm kind of a hamburger guy. . . ."

"I tried to take him hunting last night," Jade interpreted. "You know, just to show him. But he threw up."

"I didn't actually—"

"Yes, you did," Jade said calmly and cheerfully. Mark looked away. Mary-Lynnette noticed they didn't stop holding hands.

"So I take it you're not going to become a vampire," Ash said to Mark.

"Uh, let's just say not any time soon."

Ash turned to Mary-Lynnette. "And what about the human end of things? Do we have that taken care of?"

"Well, I know everything that's going on in town—by which I mean that I talked with Bunny Marten this morning. I'm so glad she's not a vampire, incidentally. . . ."

Mark said, "I always knew it."

"Anyway, here's the quick version." Mary-Lynnette held up a finger. "One, everybody knows that Jeremy is gone—his boss at the gas station missed him yesterday and went up to check the trailer. They found a lot of weird stuff there. But all they know is that he's disappeared."

"Good," Rowan said.

Mary-Lynnette held up another finger. "Two, Dad is sorry but not surprised that the station wagon blew up. Claudine has been predicting it would for a year."

Another finger. "Three, Mr. Kimble doesn't have any idea *what* killed his horse—but now he thinks it was an animal instead of a person. Vic Kimble thinks it was maybe Sasquatch. He and Todd are very spooked and want to get out of Briar Creek for good."

"And let's have a moment of silence to show how we'll miss them," Mark said solemnly, and blew a raspberry.

"Four," Mary-Lynnette said, holding up a fourth finger,

"you girls are eventually going to have to mention that your aunt hasn't come back from her 'vacation.' But I think you can wait awhile. Nobody comes out here so nobody will notice she's gone. And I think we can bury her and Jeremy safely. Even if somebody finds them, what have they got? A mummy that looks about a thousand years old and a wolf. They won't be able to connect them to the missing people."

"Poor old Aunt Opal," Jade said, still cheerful. "But she helped us in the end, didn't she?"

Mary-Lynnette looked at her. Yes, there it is, she thought. The silver in the eyes when you laugh about death. Jade is a true Night Person, too.

"She did help. And I'm going to miss her," she said out loud.

Kestrel said, "So everything is taken care of."

"Seems like it." Ash hesitated. "And Quinn is waiting down the road. I told him it would only take a couple hours to finish making arrangements and say goodbye."

There was a silence.

"I'll see you off," Mary-Lynnette said at last.

They went together to the front door. When they were outside in the twilight Ash shut the door behind them.

"You still can come with me, you know."

"With you and Quinn?"

"I'll send him away. Or I'll go and come back tomorrow and get you. Or I'll come back and stay. . . ."

"You need to go tell your father about this. Make everything right with him, so it's safe for your sisters. You *know* that."

"Well, I'll come back after *that*," Ash said, with an edge of desperation to his voice.

Mary-Lynnette looked away. The sun was gone. Looking east, the sky was already the darkest purple imaginable. Almost black. Even as she watched, a star came out. Or—not a star. Jupiter.

"I'm not ready yet. I wish I were."

"No, you don't," Ash said, and he was right, of course. She'd known ever since she sat there by the road, crying while her car burned. And although she'd thought and thought about it since then, sitting in her darkened room, there was nothing she could do to change her own mind.

She would never be a vampire. She just wasn't cut out for it. She couldn't do the things vampires had to do—and stay sane. She wasn't like Jade or Kestrel or even Rowan with her pale sinewy feet and her instinctive love of the hunt. She'd looked into the heart of the Night World . . . and she couldn't join it.

"I don't *want* you to be like that," Ash said. "I want you to be like *you*."

Without looking at him, Mary-Lynnette said, "But we're not kids. We can't be like Jade and Mark, and just hold hands and giggle and never think about the future."

"No, we're only soulmates, that's all. We're only destined to be together forever. . . ."

"If we've got forever, then you can give me time," Mary-Lynnette said. "Go back and wander a little. Take a look at the Night World and make sure you want to give it up—"

"I know that already."

"Take a look at humans and make sure you want to be tied to one of them."

"And think about the things I've done to humans, maybe?"

Mary-Lynnette looked at him directly. "Yes."

He looked away. "All right. I admit it. I've got a lot to make up for. . . ."

Mary-Lynnette knew it. He'd thought of humans as vermin—and food. The things she'd seen in his mind made her not want to picture more.

"Then make up for what you can," she said, although she didn't dare really hope that he would. "Take time to do that. And give *me* time to finish growing up. I'm still in high school, Ash."

"You'll be out in a year. I'll come back then."

"It may be too soon."

"I know. I'll come back anyway." He smiled ironically. "And in the meantime I'll fight dragons, just like any knight for his lady. I'll prove myself. You'll be proud of me."

Mary-Lynnette's throat hurt. Ash's smile disappeared. They just stood looking at each other.

It was the obvious time for a kiss. Instead, they just stood staring like hurt kids, and then one of them moved and they were holding on to each other. Mary-Lynnette held on tighter and tighter, her face buried in Ash's shoulder. Ash, who seemed to have lost it altogether, was raining kisses on the back of her neck, saying, "I wish I were a human. I wish I were."

"No, you don't," Mary-Lynnette said, seriously unsteady because of the kisses.

"I do. I do."

But it wouldn't help, and Mary-Lynnette knew he knew it. The problem wasn't simply what he was, it was what he'd done—and what he was going to do. He'd seen too much of the dark side of life to be a normal person. His nature was already formed, and she wasn't sure he could fight it.

"Believe in me," he said, as if he could hear her.

Mary-Lynnette couldn't say yes or no. So she did the only thing she could do—she lifted her head. His lips were in the right place to meet hers. The electric sparks weren't painful anymore, she discovered, and the pink haze could be quite wonderful. For a time everything was warm and sweet and strangely peaceful.

And then, behind them, somebody knocked on the door. Mary-Lynnette and Ash jumped and separated. They looked at each other, startled, emotions still too raw, and then Mary-Lynnette realized where she was. She laughed and so did Ash.

"Come out," they said simultaneously.

Mark and Jade came out. Rowan and Kestrel were behind

them. They all stood on the porch—avoiding the hole. They all smiled at Ash and Mary-Lynnette in a way that made Mary-Lynnette blush.

"Goodbye," she said firmly to Ash.

He looked at her for a long moment, then looked at the road behind him. Then he turned to go.

Mary-Lynnette watched him, blinking away tears. She still couldn't let herself believe in him. But there was no harm in hoping, was there? In wishing. Even if wishes almost never came true. . . .

Jade gasped. "Look!"

They all saw it, and Mary-Lynnette felt her heart jump violently. A bolt of light was streaking across the darkness in the northeast. Not a little wimpy shooting star—a brilliant green meteor that crossed half the sky, showering sparks. It was right above Ash's path, as if lighting his way.

A late Perseid. The last of the summer meteors. But it seemed like a blessing.

"Quick, quick, wish," Mark was telling Jade eagerly. "A wish on that star you gotta get."

Mary-Lynnette glanced at his excited face, at the way his eyes shone with excitement. Beside him, Jade was clapping, her own eyes wide with delight.

I'm so glad you're happy, Mary-Lynnette thought. My wish for you came true. So now maybe I can wish for myself.

I wish . . . I wish . . .

Ash turned around and smiled at her. "See you next year," he said. "With slain dragon!"

He started down the weed-strewn path to the road. For a moment, in the deep violet twilight, he did look to Mary-Lynnette like a knight walking off on a quest. A knight-errant with shining blond hair and no weapons, going off into a very dark and dangerous wilderness. Then he turned around and walked backward, waving, which ruined the effect.

Everyone shouted goodbyes.

Mary-Lynnette could feel them around her, her brother and her three blood-sisters, all radiating warmth and support. Playful Jade. Fierce Kestrel. Wise and gentle Rowan. And Mark, who wasn't sullen and solitary anymore. Tiggy wound himself around her ankles, purring amiably.

"Even when we're apart, we'll be looking at the same sky!" Ash yelled.

"What a line," Mary-Lynnette called back. But he was right. The sky would be there for both of them. She'd always know he was out there somewhere, looking up at it in wonder. Just knowing that was important.

And she was clear on who she was at last. She was Mary-Lynnette, and someday she'd discover a supernova or a comet or a black hole, but she'd do it as a human. And Ash would come back next year.

And she would always love the night.

The Night World lives on in *Spellbinder*, by L. J. Smith.

Expelled.

It was one of the scariest words a high school senior could think of, and it kept ringing in Thea Harman's mind as her grandmother's car approached the school building.

"This," Grandma Harman said from the front passenger seat, "is your last chance. You do realize that, don't you?"

As the driver pulled the car to the curb, she went on. "I don't know why you got thrown out of the last school, and I don't want to know. But if there's one *whiff* of trouble at this school, I'm going to give up and send both of you to your Aunt Ursula's. And you don't want *that*, now, do you?"

Thea shook her head vigorously.

Aunt Ursula's house was nicknamed the Convent, a gray fortress on a deserted mountaintop. Stone walls everywhere, an atmosphere of gloom—and Aunt Ursula watching every move with thin lips. Thea would rather die than go there.

In the backseat next to her, Thea's cousin Blaise was shaking her head, too—but Thea knew better than to hope she was listening.

Thea herself could hardly concentrate. She felt dizzy and very untogether, as if half of her were still back in New Hampshire, in the last principal's office. She kept seeing the look on his face that meant she and Blaise were about to be expelled—again.

But this time had been the worst. She'd never forget the way the police car outside kept flashing red and blue through the windows, or the way the smoke kept rising from the charred remains of the music wing, or the way Randy Marik cried as the police led him off to jail.

Or the way Blaise kept smiling. Triumphantly, as if it had all been a game.

Thea glanced sideways at her cousin.

Blaise looked beautiful and deadly, which wasn't her fault. She always looked that way; it was part of having smoldering gray eyes and hair like stopped smoke. She was as different from Thea's soft blondness as night from day and it was her beauty that kept getting them in trouble, but Thea couldn't help loving her.

After all, they'd been raised as sisters. And the sister bond was the strongest bond there was . . . to a witch.

But we can't get expelled again. We can't. *And I know you're thinking right now that you can do it all over again and good old Thea will stick with you—but this time you're wrong. This time I've got to stop you.*

"That's all," Gran said abruptly, finishing with her instructions. "Keep your noses clean until the end of October or you'll be sorry. Now, get out." She whacked the headrest of the driver's seat with her stick. "Home, Tobias."

The driver, a college-age boy with curly hair who had the dazed and beaten expression all Grandma's apprentices got after a few days, muttered, "Yes, High Lady," and reached for the gearshift. Thea grabbed for the door handle and slid out of the car fast. Blaise was right behind her.

The ancient Lincoln Continental sped off. Thea was left standing with Blaise under the warm Nevada sun, in front of the two-story adobe building complex. Lake Mead High School.

Thea blinked once or twice, trying to kick-start her brain. Then she turned to her cousin.

"Tell me," she said grimly, "that you're not going to do the same thing here."

Blaise laughed. "I never do the same thing twice."

"You know what I *mean*."

Blaise pursed her lips and reached down to adjust the top of her boot. "I think Gran overdid it a little with the lecture, don't you? I think there's something she's not telling us about. I mean, what was that bit about the end of the month?" She straightened, tossed back her mane of dark hair and smiled sweetly. "And shouldn't we be going to the office to get our schedules?"

"Are you going to answer my *question*?"

"Did you ask a question?"

Thea shut her eyes. "Blaise, we are running out of relatives. If it happens again—well, do *you* want to go to the Convent?"

For the first time, Blaise's expression darkened. Then she shrugged, sending liquid ripples down her loose ruby-colored shirt. "Better hurry. We don't want to be tardy."

"You go ahead," Thea said tiredly. She watched as her cousin walked away, hips swaying in the trademark Blaise lilt.

Thea took another breath, examining the buildings with their arched doorways and pink plaster walls. She knew the drill. Another year of living with *them*, of walking quietly through halls knowing that she was different from everybody around her, even while she was carefully, expertly pretending to be the same.

It wasn't hard. Humans weren't very smart. But it took a certain amount of concentration.

She had just started toward the office herself when she heard raised voices. A little knot of students had gathered at the edge of the parking lot.

"Stay away from it."

"Kill it!"

Thea joined the periphery of the group, being inconspicuous. But then she saw what was on the ground beyond the curb and she took three startled steps until she was looking right down at it.

Oh . . . how *beautiful.* Long, strong body . . . broad head . . . and a string of rapidly vibrating horny rings on the tail. They were making a noise like steam escaping, or melon seeds being shaken.

The snake was olive green, with wide diamonds down its back. The scales on the face looked shiny, almost wet. And its black tongue flickered so fast. . . .

A rock whizzed past her and hit the ground beside the snake. Dust puffed.

Thea glanced up. A kid in cutoffs was backing away, looking scared and triumphant.

"Don't do that," somebody said.

"Get a stick," somebody else said.

"Keep away from it."

"*Kill* it."

Another rock flew.

The faces around Thea weren't vicious. Some were curious, some were alarmed, some were filled with a sort of fascinated disgust. But it was all going to end up the same for the snake.

A boy with red hair came running up with a forked branch. People were reaching for rocks.

I can't let them, Thea thought. Rattlers were actually pretty fragile—their backbones were vulnerable. These kids might kill the snake without even meaning to.

Not to mention that a couple of the kids might get bitten in the process.

But she didn't have anything . . . no jasper against venom, no St. John root to soothe the mind.

It didn't matter. She had to do *something.* The redheaded boy was circling with the stick like a fighter looking for an opening. The kids around him were alternately warning him and cheering him on. The snake was swelling its body, tongue-tips flickering up and down faster than Thea's eye could follow. It was *mad.*

Dropping her backpack, she slipped in front of the red-haired boy. She could see his shock and she heard several people yell, but she tried to block it all out. She needed to focus.

I hope I can do this. . . .

She knelt a foot away from the rattler.

The snake fell into a striking coil. Front body raised in an S-shaped spiral, head and neck held like a poised javelin. *Nothing* looked so ready to lunge as a snake in this position.

Easy . . . easy, Thea thought, staring into the narrow catlike pupils of the yellow eyes. She slowly lifted her hands, palms facing the snake.

Worried noises from the crowd behind her.

The snake was inhaling and exhaling with a violent hiss. Thea breathed carefully, trying to radiate peace.

Now, who could help her? Of course, her own personal

protector, the goddess closest to her heart. Eileithyia of ancient Crete, the mother of the animals.

Eileithyia, Mistress of the Beasts, please tell this critter to calm *down*. Help me see into its little snaky heart so I'll know what to do.

And then it happened, the wonderful transformation that even Thea didn't understand. Part of her *became* the snake. There was a strange blurring of Thea's boundaries—she was herself, but she was also coiled on the warm ground, angry and excitable and desperate to get back to the safety of a creosote bush. She'd had eleven babies some time ago and had never quite recovered from the experience. Now she was surrounded by large, hot, fast-moving creatures.

Big-living-things . . . way too close. Not responding to my threat noises. Better bite them.

The snake had only two rules for dealing with animals that weren't food. 1) Shake your tail until they go away without stepping on you. 2) If they don't go away, strike.

Thea the person kept her hands steady and tried to pound a new thought into the small reptile brain. *Smell me. Taste me. I don't smell like a human. I'm a daughter of Hellewise.*

The snake's tongue brushed her palm. Its tips were so thin and delicate that Thea could hardly feel them flicker against her skin.

But she could feel the snake drop down from maximum alert. It was relaxing, ready to retreat. In another minute it would listen when she told it to slither away.

Behind her, she heard a new disturbance in the crowd.

"There's Eric!"

"Hey, Eric—rattlesnake!"

Block it out, Thea thought.

A new voice, distant but coming closer. "Leave it alone, guys. It's probably just a bull snake."

There was a swell of excited denial. Thea could feel her connection slipping. Stay focused. . . .

But nobody could have stayed focused during what happened next. She heard a quick footstep. A shadow fell from the east. Then she heard a gasp.

"Mojave rattler!"

And *then* something hit her, sending her flying sideways. It happened so fast that she didn't have time to twist. She landed painfully on her arm. She lost control of the snake.

All she could see as she looked east was a scaly olive-green head driving forward so fast it was a blur. Its jaws were wide open—amazingly wide—and its fangs sank into the blue-jeaned leg of the boy who had knocked Thea out of the way.